I0628270

Sherlock Holmes
and
The Portal of Time

Michael Druce

First edition published in 2017
© Copyright 2017
Michael Druce

The right of Michael Druce to be identified as the author of this
work has been asserted by him in accordance with the
Copyright, Designs and Patents Act 1998.

All rights reserved. No reproduction, copy or transmission of
this publication may be made without express prior written
permission. No paragraph of this publication may be
reproduced, copied or transmitted except with express prior
written permission or in accordance with the provisions of the
Copyright Act 1956 (as amended). Any person who commits
any unauthorized act in relation to this publication may be
liable to criminal prosecution and civil claims for damage.

All characters appearing in this work are fictitious or used
fictitiously. Except for certain historical personages, any
resemblance to real persons, living or dead, is purely
coincidental. The opinions expressed herein are those of the
author and not of MX Publishing.

Paperback ISBN 978-1-78705-052-5
ePub ISBN 978-1-78705-053-2
PDF ISBN 978-1-78705-054-9

Published in the UK by MX Publishing
335 Princess Park Manor, Royal Drive,
London, N11 3GX
www.mxpublishing.co.uk

Cover design by Brian Belanger.

"Randall's Folly image used with permission of Town of
Salthouse www.salthousehistory.co.uk"

FORWARD

Faithful readers of my chronicles of Sherlock Holmes will note an unfamiliar narrative approach to this work. The scope of this particular story necessitates that I render some events, thoughts, and conversations that I was not personally party to. As such I now assume the role of all-knowing author. Through painstaking research and interviews, I have tried for accuracy as faithfully as possible. In cases where fidelity was not possible, I have taken dramatic license.

John H. Watson

CHAPTER 1
Past is prologue

It began with a volley of gunfire!

As 1918 drew to a close, London was a city in ruin. The Great War of 1914 officially ended the previous month on the eleventh of November, fueling hopes for a future without the specter of more wars. It grieves me to report that was a hope not to be realized. The rebuilding of our glorious city commenced almost immediately after the armistice with a passion unlike any I had witnessed before. Our tiny island had remained impervious to conventional attack. The invaders had not been able to cross the channel and assault us by land. Instead, their assault came by way of a far more insidious means. It came silently at night by air. The Germans unleashed on London warfare by way of zeppelin. The devastation of the German aerial bombing campaign was staggering. Those leviathans of the air sliced silently through the night skies bombing with indiscriminate effectiveness, if not precision. The bombing was intended to be strategic, but most often the bombs missed their marks and destroyed buildings of no military value. London's notorious fogs often obscured the targets the zeppelins were seeking. Gradually bombers took the places of the zeppelins. In the years that followed, thousands would lose their lives to these death machines from the sky and London would be a city wounded, but not defeated. England's enemies had been formidable to be sure, but we had yet to face the enemy that could crush our spirit and resolve.

Much that had been familiar and comforting to Londoners had been reduced to rubble. Many of the familiar haunts Sherlock Holmes and I would often frequent were either severely damaged or no longer existed. At night one could lull oneself into pretending London was at it had always been, but come dawn the destruction of this ancient and beloved city was all too apparent. Holmes and I did our part throwing ourselves into helping and rebuilding wherever the need. It was an exhausting time but one filled with energy and the conviction that the empire had withstood the onslaught. Her spirit was unmatched. It was truly heartening to see a strong, proud people rise up and rebuild. There would always be an England.

Seventy miles from London Herbert George Wells staggered through the door of his cottage in Sandgate. He knocked over the umbrella stand near the door, stumbled toward his favorite chair and collapsed into it, exhausted. His collar had sprung open, his tie askew, vest unbuttoned, and his hair in disarray. He might have looked the part of a man who had spent the weekend carousing, wandering from one pub to the next, were it not for the blood stain on the back of his left trouser leg.

Jane Wells, his devoted wife, was in the kitchen scrubbing a pot. Immediately she stopped the task at hand and hurried to the front room. Her husband was splayed out in his chair, perspiration streaming down his forehead. His breathing was labored.

"Bertie, Bertie, my goodness. What has happened?"

"Hello, darling." Wells said weakly. The words were almost too much to get out.

Jane Wells was simply aghast. "You're absolutely drenched with perspiration. I'll get you a wet cloth." She hurried back to the kitchen, immersed a clean dish cloth under the tap and returned to her exhausted husband." She patted the wet cloth against Wells' forehead. "You must tell me where you have been. What has happened?"

"I told you, I had some business in Scotland."

Jane undid her husband's tie and pulled it through his collar. She unbuttoned the first two eyelets of his shirt and pulled it open. "Here," she said, handing him an envelope from the table, "fan yourself with this."

Wells did as he was told, thankful for the cool air.

"You're so disheveled. You look positively worn out. Are you all right?"

"No, actually, I am not. I have been shot." Wells turned his left leg, revealing the dried bloodstain on his calf.

"What?" Jane gasped. "You're bleeding!"

"Yes, I've been shot. I was nicked in the leg. It's nothing serious."

"Nothing serious? You've been shot. I am calling the police." Jane hurried to the telephone and began tapping the drop hook. "Hello, hello. Operator!"

Wells tried to rise from his chair, but his wounded leg would not cooperate. It could bear no more weight. He fell back spent. "No, please Jane, you mustn't call the police. Be a good girl and do as I say."

Jane replaced the receiver and turned sharply to her husband. "Bertie, please do not call me a good girl. That sounds patronizing and you know how I dislike that."

"Yes, yes," Wells said. "I'm sorry. I am out of sorts."

"Tell me why I should not call the police."

"It's a bit complicated, actually. I wonder if I might have a drink."

"Of course." Jane went to the cupboard where the spirits are kept and removed a decanter of sherry and one glass. She poured a liberal measure of sherry, placed the decanter and the glass on a silver service tray and set it next to her husband. "Here you are."

Wells ignored the glass and drank directly from the decanter.

"You've done something wrong! I know you have."

Jane's tone was all too familiar. She was not asking a question. It was incumbent on Wells to explain himself.

"As I said, it is complicated."

"You really *have* done something wrong." Jane snatched the glass filled with sherry from the table and gulped it down. She went into the bathroom and returned with a first aid kit. "Here, let me look at that. Drop your trousers."

Wells hadn't the strength to disobey. He struggled to his feet, removed his jacket and vest and loosened his braces, letting his trousers fall to the floor. Jane knelt and set about sanitizing the wound.

"This is temporary. I shall want the doctor to look at it. Now, tell me what you have done."

"It is nothing criminal, it's just a bit hard to explain."

"Why are you being evasive? It is 1918. These kinds of things don't happen in civilized society. Tell me who shot you or I shall telephone Scotland Yard immediately."

"No, a thousand times no. If I tell, will you promise not to go to the police?" Wells downed another mouthful of sherry.

Jane sat back on her heels. "I promise. But you must tell me the truth."

"Very well. I traveled to Berlin several years into the future and I was accosted by a group of soldiers who called themselves Nazis. There, now you have it."

Jane drenched the cleansing gauze with alcohol and pressed it hard against the wound. Wells let out a cry.

"Serves you right. I am calling the police."

"No, you said you wouldn't!"

"Herbert, why would you tell me such a story? I am your wife. I will not be treated as a child."

The wound was now clean enough to wrap. Jane applied a bandage and wrapped a plaster around her husband's calf.

"You will need to bathe before we see the doctor. I'll bring your dressing gown."

Jane went into the bedroom and removed a well-worn dressing gown from the wardrobe.

"Yes, you're quite right." Wells undid his shirt and folded it over the back of his chair. "I don't know what came over me. It was a frightful experience."

"You said Germany."

"Did I?"

"Yes, you said Germany."

"I meant Scotland. The whole thing's clouded my thinking. I've been working on that new novel—and, well, I was some place--in Scotland--that I shouldn't have been. I got lost and bumped into a gang of thugs with whom I got cross ways with."

"These men, where did you meet them? Who were they?" Jane helped her husband into his dressing gown.

"I can't be sure. It was a tavern—"

"A tavern?"

"Did I say tavern? I mean pub. It was a pub."

"It was a pub. I believe you. Go on."

"It's all rather hazy. They were a nasty bunch, combative fellows. They called themselves Nazis."

A blank expression came over Jane's face. "What is a Nazi?"

"I don't know. Perhaps it is some sort of gang moniker."

"Why didn't you go to the police?"

"I should have, only my leg was killing me. Well, you know the Scots. I thought the whole thing would drag on. I just wanted to come home as quickly as possible. My injury appears worse than it is."

"It's a wonder you didn't bleed to death. Did you accomplish what you intended?" Jane cleared up the mess her husband's wound had created. She threw the bloodstained bandages and ruined trousers into the rubbish bin.

"What's that?" Wells was coming over lightheaded from the sherry.

"Your business in Scotland! The research for your sequel to *The Time Machine.* Did you discover what you were looking for?"

"Yes."

Writing as H.G. Wells, Herbert George Wells enjoyed immense success writing science fiction. He shared the appellation The Father of Modern Science with the late Jules Verne as well as Hugo Gernsback, a successful writer, inventor, and a contemporary. *The Time Machine* was the first in a succession of novels that would cement Wells' reputation. Well in advance of World War I, Wells had published a lesser-known novel entitled *The War in the Air.* As I had done with my own adventures of Sherlock Holmes published in *The Strand*, Wells had published *The War in the Air* in serial form. His story appeared in the pages of *Pall Mall Magazine.* The work proved eerily prophetic in that it anticipated the use of flying machines as a weapon of war. One could not fail to recall Wells' prescience when the Germans began their deadly zeppelin campaign.

For my part, science fiction, or science romance as it was originally called, held little interest. As a man of medicine intimately involved with a man of science and deduction, the writings of Wells and those of others seemed little more than frippery to me. I much preferred the world of hard science to that of science fantasy.

Satisfied that Wells was out of immediate medical danger, Jane Wells placed a chair opposite her husband. "I wonder if your research is connected with the man who came to visit while you were away?"

The expression on Wells' face changed. He immediately became clear headed. "There was a man? What man? Who?"

Jane thought for a moment. "I don't know who. He didn't give me a name. He came to the door two nights ago. It was dark. I thought it most unusual someone knocking so late."

"What did he say? What did he want?"

"He apologized for intruding at such a late hour. He inquired as to whether or not you were home. He said he had sat in on a couple of your lectures and wondered if he might have a word with you."

"You didn't recognize him? Had you ever seen him before?"

"No, I don't know him, nor have I ever seen him before. I explained you were away on a short trip to Scotland."

"Can you describe this man?"

"I don't know. It was dark. It was very hard to see. He wore his coat buttoned up to his chin, and his hat was pulled down low. He wore dark glasses."

"He was wearing dark glasses at night?"

"Yes, I thought that was quite odd. He reminded me of that fellow from your novel *The Invisible Man*."

"Is that all?"

"Yes, he didn't remind me of any other characters."

"What I mean is there anything else you remember about him?"

"Do you have some reason to be concerned about this man?"

Wells suddenly found himself becoming short tempered with his wife. "That couldn't have been all. There must have been something else you recall."

"A cane! Yes, I remember now. He walked with a cane. He had a limp. Do you know him?"

"No!" Wells' mind began to race. "He must have given some reason for wanting to see me! Think Jane, think!"

"I am trying, but you are making me very nervous."

Wells reached for his wife's hand.

"Yes, now I recall. He asked where you do your writing."

Wells' heart fluttered.

"I told him in the cottage behind the main house. He thanked me, apologized for the lateness of the hour and bid me goodnight."

"You told him that?"

"Yes. It seemed an innocent question. Was that wrong?"

"Oh, my goodness." Wells gripped the arms of the chair and rose shakily to his feet. He hopped toward the front door, took an umbrella from the overturned umbrella stand and hopscotched unsteadily through the door, using the umbrella as a makeshift cane.

"Herbert, you are not dressed!" Jane cried. Clearly something was amiss. She went to the sideboard where the spirits were kept and sorted through a handful of telephone books. Removing the London telephone book, she quickly thumbed through the pages until she found the number she was searching for. She pressed the telephone receiver to her ear and quickly tapped the drop hook. "Yes, thank you. Would you please connect me with Mayfair 7459? Yes, of course, I'll wait." She hung the receiver on the drop hook and began to pace.

A moment later Wells hobbled back inside, gesticulating wildly. "The cottage has been broken into, the place has been positively ransacked. My papers are missing."

"Your novel?" Jane gasped. "Your novel has been taken?"

"No, my research! I am completely undone. My scientific notes are gone."

The telephone rang suddenly. Before Jane could make a move, Wells snatched up the receiver. "Hello!" He barked into the telephone. He listened for a moment and then covered the mouthpiece with his hand. He turned toward his wife. "I said no police. Jane, you promised."

"You said no police." And then with a hint of self-satisfaction she added, "You didn't say I couldn't telephone Sherlock Holmes."

CHAPTER 2
Deja vu

By 1921, London was bustling and well on the mend. She still bore the scars of the war, but her convalescence was nearing an end. Life for most Londoners had returned to a semblance of those pre-war years. My time was devoted to my medical practice and I continued to chronicle the adventures of my friend Sherlock Holmes. The Great Detective was never happier than when immersed in a challenging case.

On this particular morning, I let myself into 221 B Baker Street without knocking. I was as much a fixture at that address as the full time residents themselves. I climbed the stairs to the apartment above and bid good morning to Mrs. Hudson, Holmes' indispensable housekeeper. She greeted me in her usual cheerful manner and said she would announce me.

"Come in Mrs. Hudson," Holmes said before Mrs. Hudson could knock on the apartment door.

Mrs. Hudson opened the door slowly and poked her head inside. Holmes was concealed behind a copy of *The London Times*. "I don't mean to disturb you, Mr. Holmes—"

"Then don't."

"Begging your pardon, Mr. Holmes?"

Holmes folded the newspaper and set it beside the breakfast dishes on the small table beside his Chesterfield club chair. "Mrs. Hudson, if you don't mean to disturb me, then you shouldn't. Clearly, you meant to. Now that you have, please show Dr. Watson in."

"But, but Mr. Holmes," Mrs. Hudson blustered, "I've not said anything about Dr. Watson."

"It wasn't necessary. There was a squeak on the left hand side of the third step. Dr. Watson is the only person I know who navigates the stairs to my apartment on the left hand side."

One doesn't share a residence with Sherlock Holmes without occasionally attempting to find fault with one of his deductions. "Yes, but couldn't someone else use the left side of the stairs?" Mrs. Hudson inquired.

"Of course, they could; however, since we heard no buzzer, that meant our guest was familiar enough with my residence to enter without formally announcing himself. Who, other than Dr. Watson, might that be?"

Mrs. Hudson shook her head in amazement. "You are a wonder, Mr. Holmes."

"Yes, I know."

"Will there be anything--?"

"No thank you, Mrs. Hudson. If you will clear away the breakfast things, that will be all."

Mrs. Hudson removed the breakfast dishes from the small table and opened the door to Holmes' apartment for me. "Come in, Dr. Watson."

"Mrs. Hudson, you really should do something about that—"

"Third step? Yes, I know, it squeaks. I'll have it looked into. Good day, Doctor."

"What? Oh, yes." I alighted in the chair opposite my good friend. "Remarkable, Holmes, remarkable!"

"What's that, Watson?" Holmes was preparing his first pipe of the day.

"Mrs. Hudson seems to have remarkable powers of deduction. She knew what I was going to say before I said it. Must come from being your housekeeper."

"What other explanation could there be?" Holmes struck a match and lit the shag tobacco in his black clay pipe.

"Quite right."

Here, dear reader, I must interrupt our narrative and offer a fuller accounting of myself. In chronicling these adventures, it was never my intent to portray myself as what has become known in contemporary parlance as the comic sidekick. In order to fully amplify Holmes deductive skills, it has been necessary for me to play the role of foil, one who is never quite in step with Holmes and who asks the questions readers themselves are curious about. As a result of numerous iterations of our adventures on stage and in film, I am afraid Dr. Watson has become a caricature. He is, lacking a better way to describe my fictional self, a slightly befuddled wag. After adventures in every imaginable medium, I unfortunately have no choice but to play that role, which I am sure accounts for the fair number of readers I meet who remark that I am quite different from the Dr. Watson they had imagined. In that same vein, our good friend Inspector Lestrade of Scotland Yard has also become a caricature. I sincerely apologize to the good inspector. But more about Lestrade later.

It was as that decidedly droll version of myself that I said to Holmes, "Looking over *The Times*, I see. Anything of interest?"

An all too familiar twinkle appeared in Holmes' eyes and a hint of excitement in his voice. "As a matter fact there is something of interest. Déjà vu, Watson. Know anything about it?"

"French, isn't it?"

"Yes! Déjà vu, Watson. Know anything about it?"

Holmes wasn't the kind to pull one's leg. I wasn't sure what to make of his repeating what he had just asked. "Er—yes--the feeling that you are experiencing something that has happened before."

"I suddenly experienced it reading through today's paper." He handed me the paper folded up on the side table. "Two stories have caught my eye. The first is about an extraordinary scientist from Germany. He has been lecturing at Manchester for the summer, sharing some unique and controversial theories about space, time, and physics. He was scheduled to travel to America yesterday with H.G. Wells."

"Wells?" That name had a familiar ring, but as I paid little attention to the science fiction community, that was not the source of my familiarity. Then it came to me. "That science fiction chap who wouldn't speak with us. What was it, two years ago?"

"Three years ago."

"There you are then, that explains your déjà vu."

"No, it is something else, something I cannot put my finger on." Holmes pressed two fingers against his left temple as if he might divine the answer to the problem he was grappling with.

"What is our friend H. G. Wells up to these days?"

"Wells and the young scientist were scheduled to do a series of lectures on the relationship between science fiction and science fact."

"That scientist fellow should keep away from Wells." I chortled. "Science fiction is a lot of mumbo jumbo."

"I beg to differ, old chap. Scientific theory and fact often begin in the realm of the fanciful."

"Invisible men, invaders from Mars, and time machines, indeed." I couldn't imagine Holmes giving credence to such silliness.

Holmes rose and went to the globe of the Earth standing in the corner of the room. He spun the sphere with his long, slender fingers. "Much of what was once regarded as science fiction is today reality. Case in point, Jules Verne, a man of remarkable vision and clarity."

"Holmes, surely a man of your intellectual gifts sees those stories as nothing more than the product of a vivid imagination."

"I think you underestimate Mr. Wells, Watson. The scientific community looks rather favorably on his works. You recall his uncanny vision of the future of warfare in *The War in the Air*."

"If you recall—I think it was two years ago—"

Holmes pressed his fingers against the spinning globe and stopped it cold. "No, Watson, it was three."

"Speaking of déjà vu."

"Yes, that mysterious visit to the Wells home in Sandgate."

"Some sort of wild goose chase, if memory serves."

"Precisely my thoughts at the time, but time and perspective can change one's opinion."

"Really? After two--three years?"

"Given my current feelings, I feel it is worth recalling that meeting."

CHAPTER 3
Visitors

The telephone call came as so many of our famous cases did, unexpectedly and sounded as anything but extraordinary. I was never sure how Holmes decided to look into a case. Try as I might, I was unable to discern any rhyme or reason. It was as the French say, *je ne sais quoi*. Whatever it was, it would strike a responsive chord deep within and off we'd go.

Soon after Holmes took the call, we were on the train to Sandgate. As Wells was something of a celebrity, the rather incomplete directions supplied by Mrs. Wells were of little consequence. Everyone knew where the most famous resident of Sandgate resided.

Mrs. Wells greeted us with a friendly smile and a hint of trepidation. "Thank you for coming on such short notice, Mr. Holmes. I am Amy Wells. My friends and my husband call me Jane."

"Allow me to introduce my colleague, Dr. Watson."

"How do you do, Mrs. Wells?"

"I trust you are well, Mr. Holmes. I read about your—"

"Accident," Holmes interjected quickly, as if he wished to forestall any further discussion along those lines.

"Accident, indeed," I chimed in. The experience had been all too visceral for me. I wasn't ready to dismiss it so easily. It was practically a battle to the death with Professor Moriarty at Reichenbach Falls. Holmes was lucky to have survived. As to the Professor, his remains were never found. The violent, churning falls gave up no secrets.

"Please, Watson, we are not here to discuss me."

"I am glad you have regained your health, Mr. Holmes."

"Fully recovered, thank you."

"Walked with a cane for months."*

"Now, Mrs. Wells, the fact that your husband is not by your side suggests to me that he chooses not to speak with us. This matter of great urgency is not shared by Mr. Wells, I take it."

"Whether Herbert will admit it or not, I think my husband is in grave danger."

"From whom? How? Why?"

"I am not sure, Doctor. I haven't been able to piece it all together."

"Has someone threatened your husband?" Holmes asked.

"As I related to you on the telephone, he went on a short trip to Scotland. When he returned he was completely out of sorts. He wouldn't tell me much. What he did tell me was vague at best."

"Could it have been related to his injury?"

"His injury? How do you know about that?"

"Elementary, my dear Mrs. Wells. We—Mr. Holmes--observed a pair of crutches in the entry hall."

"Herbert sustained a gunshot wound to the leg. He said he ran into a gang of thugs."

"Probably nothing more than a bit of bad luck, in the wrong place at the wrong time." I couldn't imagine Holmes saw more to this than I.

"What had your husband been doing during the time leading up to the incident?"

"Writing, lecturing. As a science fiction writer, Herbert has an extensive knowledge of science. He does all of his writing and research in the cottage behind the main house. He is very secretive about it. He claims all of his work has a scientific basis."

"Poppycock!" I chortled impulsively.

"Watson!"

"Sorry, bit of a cough."

"Continue, please."

"As a result of his research, the university has asked him to do some lectures on the theories he has been working on for his new novel."

"A new novel, you say?"

"Yes, he says it's a sequel to *The Time Machine.* He hasn't let me read the drafts yet. The rest you know from our telephone conversation."

"Over the telephone you gave a brief but not especially useful description of a stranger who came to your door. Was there anything distinctive in his voice? Anything you might have noticed. His posture? His walk?"

My sense was that Holmes continued to ask questions as a matter of courtesy. We had been colleagues long enough that I usually had a good feel for his interest. This investigation would surely come to naught.

"Since speaking with you, I made some notes about that night." Mrs. Wells retrieved a small black notebook from the bureau and quickly leafed through it. "I don't recall anything distinctive about his voice, but he did use a cane. He had quite a pronounced limp."

"Your husband knew this man?"

"Mrs. Wells closed the notebook. No. He said he had no idea who he was."

"And yet he didn't want to involve the police," I interjected.

"That is correct. He was most adamant."

Holmes stood motionless with his fingers steepled against his chin in a pose of prayerful contemplation. I had witnessed this pose on many occasions. He was deep in thought. Any moment he would spring to life with a series of insights. Abruptly the steepled fingers dropped to his side. "I am afraid there isn't anything we can do. If your husband refuses to involve the police and he does not wish to speak with me, we have nothing to go on."

Clearly, this was not what Mrs. Wells was expecting. "My husband is a stubborn man, Mr. Holmes."

"Foolish, I'd say." Thinking better of my response, I amended it to, "Perhaps not foolish, perhaps—"

"Fearful." Holmes said.

"There is one other thing." Mrs. Wells opened the small black notebook again. "Yes, here it is. I made a note of it because I thought it odd. This gang of thugs he claims that shot him. He said they called themselves Nazis. Does that name mean anything to either of you?"

Holmes and I glanced at each other for a moment. Simultaneously we arrived at the same answer. "No!"

That concluded our visit to Sandgate. H.G. Wells had no wish to see us, and Jane Wells had told us everything she knew. The case warranted no further attention.

*Contradictory accounts of what actually happened at Reichenbach Falls exist in my own chronicles and those reported elsewhere. At the request of my editors, *The Adventure of the Empty House* has Holmes deceiving everyone into believing that he did not actually descend into the falls. The general opinion held that surviving such a fall seemed unlikely. For the purposes of this adventure, I have chosen not to maintain that artifice.

CHAPTER 4
A visitor comes to 221 B

"There you have it. Our visit to Sandgate served no purpose. Here we are three years later and Wells is on his way to America with this German chap."

Holmes crossed to the window and looked toward the sky. A breeze rustled the curtains. Rain was moving in. Thunder rumbled in the distance along with an occasional flash of lightning.

"I fail to see the relevance of revisiting that wasted journey, unless of course you will want to attend one of his lectures once he returns."

"Precisely, Watson, were it not for the fact that he has been kidnapped."

"What? H.G. Wells kidnapped?"

"No, Watson. Wells is quite safe at home. He has cancelled his trip to America. It is his fellow lecturer I am speaking of."

"The German chap? What did you say his name is?"

"I didn't say, but his name is Einstein. Albert Einstein."

"Einstein?" I vaguely recalled reading about him the papers, but frankly I paid little attention. I hardly knew much about him at all. "Isn't he the relativity fellow?"

From below came the sound of the front door buzzer.

Holmes turned enthusiastically to me. "You are about to learn a great deal more. The lady being shown in by Mrs. Hudson is about to fill us in."

"Lady?"

"Unlike you, Watson, she navigates the right hand side of the stairs, thus no creak on the third step. Red dress, I would say, fashionable bonnet and long white gloves."

"What?" I blustered.

Then came the knock on the apartment door.

"And a parasol."

Without question, Holmes had skills far more advanced than the average person, but I did not count clairvoyance among them. "How could you possibly know that from a knock on the door?"

"Elementary, my dear Watson, I saw the lady just now from the window. She was comparing the address with a card in her hand."

"Come in, Mrs. Hudson."

"Mr. Holmes, there's a lady—"

"Yes, thank you, Mrs. Hudson, that will be all."

Mrs. Hudson stepped aside to allow our guest to enter and then exited.

"Come in, Mrs. Einstein."

Both our guest and I were taken aback as the lady had not yet been introduced.

"But I—"

"I am afraid your photograph in *The Times* does not do you justice."

"You are most kind, Mr. Holmes."

"Allow me to introduce my colleague, Dr. Watson.

"How do you do? Won't you please have a seat?"

Our guest accepted my offer. I also sat, but Holmes remained standing. He did this whenever his interest was peaked. His energy could only be harnessed by moving. "How may we help you, Mrs. Einstein?"

"You are familiar with my husband?"

"Of course. I read the story in this morning's *Times.*"

"Then you know why I have come. One day before we were to set sail for America, my husband vanished."

"Vanished? But Holmes, I thought you said Einstein was kidnapped."

"One in the same, Watson. *The Times* has provided a full account. You may read about it later. Now, Mrs. Einstein, what satisfaction have you received from Inspector Lestrade and Scotland Yard?"

"None whatsoever, he has been of no help at all."

Before I recount Mrs. Einstein's meeting with Inspector Lestrade, I must set the record straight. I feel partly responsible in some measure for contributing to the general impression that our good friend the Inspector is both a comical and largely inept individual. Here again, stage and film interpretations of the Inspector have done him an injustice. To my earlier point, the abilities Holmes possesses can only be fully appreciated when comparing him with others of lesser capabilities. Lestrade is, in fact, a wholesome and dedicated individual. While it is true he has called on the services of Sherlock Holmes and me on numerous occasions, it is worth remembering the notorious cases Holmes has taken on throughout the years number in the dozens, whereas Lestrade's case load, whether a case of little consequence or one of considerable notoriety, numbers in the hundreds, perhaps even thousands. Holmes has enjoyed the luxury of taking on only those cases that interest him. As a representative of Scotland Yard, Inspector Lestrade is not at liberty to pick and choose cases.

Based upon what Mrs. Einstein shared with Holmes and me, Lestrade can easily be forgiven for not proving to be of more help.

"After sharing everything I knew, Inspector Lestrade seemed dismissive. He said I hadn't given him much to work with."

"You are quite sure you told him everything?" Holmes asked.

"Two men jumped from a car, apprehended my husband, and sped away."

"How did the inspector respond?"

"He asked if I could identify the car."

"Were you able to identify it?"

"Yes, I told him it was black."

Holmes moved to the window and looked down at the seemingly endless flow of black vehicles creeping along Baker Street in the downpour. "How did the inspector respond?"

"He said, 'Black, eh? Well, that certainly narrows it down. They could be anywhere by now, couldn't they?'"

"I told him I couldn't possibly know that as I am not a police detective. Then he asked about a ransom note. I told him there was none. He thought that seemed odd, but he felt sure whoever is responsible would soon make an appearance and demand a cash ransom. He allowed that when that moment came, he would be there to nab those *pikers*, as he referred to them."

"Hardly pikers," I offered. This felt too premeditated to be the work of a casual kidnapping.

"And so you thought to come to see me."

"I didn't know where else to turn, Mr. Holmes."

"You were quite right in coming here."

"You will help me then. Can you find my husband, Mr. Holmes?"

"At the moment no, but I can assure you no harm will come to him."

"How can you provide that assurance?"

"There was no ransom involved, so there can be no threat of harm if payment is not made."

"I see," Mrs. Einstein said.

"What Mr. Holmes means is a man of knowledge and expertise is more valuable alive than—"

"I beg to differ. Mr. Einstein has written numerous papers and he is currently lecturing at Cambridge. What he knows is easily obtainable without resorting to kidnapping. No, there is something else."

"But what?" Mrs. Einstein asked, exhibiting for the first time since she had arrived a keener interest in the direction of the conversation.

"That is what I hope to eventually learn."

"You said there is nothing you can do."

"For the time being, there isn't. Go home, Mrs. Einstein. Take comfort. Your husband will be released soon, I am sure of that. When he is fully restored, have him pay me a visit. Mrs. Hudson will show you out."

"Thank you, Mr. Holmes. I do hope you are right."

I rose and opened the door for Mrs. Einstein.

"Good day, Doctor."

"Good day, Mrs. Einstein."

As I was about to close the door behind our guest, she paused and turned back. "Forgive me, Mr. Holmes, one last question."

"Of course."

"I wonder if you have discussed this matter with Whitehall?"

Holmes did not immediately answer. I directed a glance toward him. Had he not heard Mrs. Einstein's question? "Holmes?"

"No, I have not." Holmes said, as if he had snapped out of a fugue.

"Good day, Mr. Holmes. Doctor."

I closed the door behind our guest and turned to Holmes. "I must say, Holmes, that's not like you to leave a young woman in distress. Can you be sure the motive is not murder?"

"The body would already have been found floating in the Thames. With the exception of today, this has been an unusually hot summer. No one could afford to keep a body on ice."

"Yes, I suppose you are right. I am curious about one thing, however. Why do you think Mrs. Einstein asked if you had discussed her husband's disappearance with Whitehall? Hadn't you only just learned of his disappearance this morning?"

"Yes, Watson, my thought exactly. I expect we shall learn more when Mr. Einstein pays a visit."

"Should he determine to pay us a visit."

"He will pay us a visit all right. One of the greatest minds in the world will surely not pass up an opportunity to meet another of the greatest minds in the world."

At times Holmes could be insufferable. "Yes, quite so. You've got me curious now. I'm looking forward to meeting this fellow."

"I think our conversation will prove most illuminating."

There was a knock on the door, followed by a crack of thunder and flash of lightning.

"Come in, Mrs. Hudson."

The door swung open. Mrs. Hudson entered with a tea service. "My, oh, my, it's getting nasty out there. Tea, Mr. Holmes?"

"Yes, thank you."

Mrs. Hudson arranged the tea service on the table.

"Don't you think it's odd, Holmes, that the same thing that happened to Einstein happened to Wells? They both disappeared."

"Not at all, Watson. The cases are quite dissimilar. If you recall, Mr. Wells announced to his wife he would be going on a short journey. Mr. Einstein has been abducted. Yet the two cases are intriguing, especially when one juxtaposes them with this small story on page five of *The Times*."

"Oh, what's that?" Clearly, there was much to read in the day's paper.

"Another vagabond has disappeared."

"Another?"

"Oh, I read that story," Mrs. Hudson chimed in.

"Over the past several years there has been a series of disappearances. Mostly vagabonds, but not all."

One heard about such things from time to time. People just up and vanished. Usually there was a plausible explanation. Some people just wanted to disappear. Other cases proved more baffling. As a result of imaginations fired by the works of H G. Wells and other writers, an idea gaining currency among certain individuals was something being referred to as *paleo-abductions*.

"About a dozen recorded incidents," Holmes continued. "Sometimes alone, sometimes in pairs. Most intriguing."

"You don't suppose it's the return of Jack the Ripper, do you? My, that was a wicked terrible time."

"No," I gently reproved. "By now The Ripper would be well into old age."

"For reasons that evade me, I feel these disappearances are somehow related to the disappearance of Professor Einstein and the incident involving Mr. Wells and his shadowy guest."

"These incidents are three years apart. That's quite a stretch. What evidence do you have?"

"None, whatsoever. Call it a hunch."

"A hunch? Holmes, that's not at all like you. These other disappearances, where have they taken place? Here in London?"

"No, Watson, somewhere in Scotland."

CHAPTER 5
The Stones

Well North of the boundary that separates Scotland from England, the tiny village of Loch Naire may be found. Unlike most villages up and down the rail line that links Edinburg with London, Loch Naire has little to recommend in the way of amenities for the travel weary. It is little more than a coal and water stop for trains traveling either to or from Edinburg. Travelers rarely disembark as the village center is too far to walk and neither buses nor cabs service the station. The station itself is little more than a ticket office, a waiting room, and toilet facilities. Were Loch Naire a song, it would be a dirge.

Some few dozen meters beyond the end of the platform following the trajectory of the rail line north may be found a thicket in the middle of which is a small clearing. The clearing is hardly large enough to accommodate a dozen men standing in close proximity. Its only remarkable feature is a pair of unexpectedly massive boulders that appear to have been blasted from the bowels of the Earth millions of years earlier. Juxtaposed as they are, the boulders form what at first glance appears to be a cave between them. Upon closer inspection it becomes clear there is no cave at all, but an alcove less than two meters deep, easy enough to stand in but providing no shelter from the elements. Locals know the spot as The Stones, but rare is the visitor. Throughout the centuries strange markings informed by ancient rituals have contributed to a lore of the unexplained and mysterious, which contributes to a sinister aspect that keeps most people away. Other than the occasional gypsy and vagabond who use the spot to wait for passing freighters to ferry them to and from the network of towns and villages up and down the railway system, The Stones exist in virtual seclusion. Once in a while a passing vagabond might decamp in the clearing by day for easy access to the station's toilet facilities or at night to sleep on one of the station's benches unhampered by night creatures, but few stay long. One must always keep an eye open for the local Station Inspector who does not take kindly to vagrants sacked out on the benches.

This cold, moonless night a thick fog rolled in. A pair of weary vagrants were doing their best to stay warm while awaiting the arrival of the next coal train on its way north. Rabbie, the eldest of the two tramps, started a fire in an old metal barrel that had been dragged into the clearing years ago. The cold was biting as he gathered twigs and branches and anything else that might burn. The old man lugged a rotting log to the barrel and heaved it inside. It hit bottom with such a clatter, that his mate Broden sprang awake on the station bench a few meters away.

"Rabbie, is that you?" the startled tramp cried out.

"Yeah, mate. It's all right, not to worry. I just dropped a chunk of wood into the barrel." He stirred the contents of the barrel with a broken limb.

Broden sat up and rubbed his hands together. The flicker of the fire burned brightly through the thicket. This could be a fearful place at night. The dancing shadows produced by the fire did nothing to disabuse the tramp of that notion. "We better get a move on. " He called out to his friend in the clearing. "If the Station Inspector sees that fire, he'll be on us. It's about time for his rounds."

"It's wicked cold, I tell you. A night in jail might be just the thing." Rabbie held his hands over the fire.

"You don't need to tell me. Me nose is about to drop off."

"I'd give anything for a bit of warmth."

In the distance Broden glimpsed a small light moving up the lane toward the station. Only one person would be cycling this time of night. "Heads up," he called to his friend. "Station Inspector."

"Blast!" Rabbie groaned as he backed away from the fire toward the two massive stones. "I'd rather be anywhere but here."

A moment later there was a flash of light followed by a swooshing noise.

Broden gauged the distance of the Station Inspector and grabbed his knapsack. "No good wishing your life away." He hopped off the end of the platform and made his way through the thicket into the clearing. "Better put that fire—" Broden stopped mid-sentence. Rabbie was nowhere to be seen. "Hello? Hey, mate! Rabbie? Rabbie?"

Twigs snapped on the ground behind him. Broden turned. The Station Inspector had discovered them.

"You two, again. Come on move along! No loitering about. Where's your mate then? Where's he hiding?"

Broden scratched his head. Near the base of the stones lay a smoldering limb. "I don't know. I was just speaking to him. He's— he's gone. Vanished!"

"Vanished," the Station Inspector harrumphed. "Right, then make like him and be off."

"He was here I tell you. I was just having a word with him."

"Grab a handful of dirt and smother that fire. And pick up that smoldering bit of wood there." The Station Inspector pushed his way out of the thicket. He rubbed his hands together and waited for the vagrant to come out. The flames died down to an orange glow. He was becoming impatient. "Come on then, I don't have all night."

Suddenly there was a flash of light and a swooshing sound.

"Hello? Hello?" The Station Inspector pushed his way back through the thicket and into the clearing. He scoured the area with his torch. There was no one there. "Blimey," he muttered to himself. "He's vanished!"

CHAPTER 6
The man from Berlin

As Sherlock Holmes predicted, Albert Einstein came calling. Well before his visit to 221 B Baker Street, Einstein's reputation as one of the world's leading physicists was firmly established. Some few years earlier he had published his groundbreaking paper on general relativity. For most individuals, myself among them, his work was far too abstruse to comprehend with any degree of confidence. As best I could fathom, Einstein postulated that Sir Isaac Newton's laws of classical mechanics, a set of physical laws describing the motion of bodies influenced by force, were no longer adequate to explain the laws of electro-magnetics. A new method of conceptualizing electromagnetic forces and gravity was necessary, which led to investigations into quantum theory, particle theory, and the motion of molecules. Eventually Einstein's research would lead to a consideration of time as it related to energy, mass, and the speed of light.

The brilliant young scientist sat in the same chair as his wife had a few days earlier. Holmes listened politely to our guest's brief digression as he filled us in on his scientific achievements. I knew Holmes well enough to know he had no interest whatsoever in Einstein's scientific work. His sole interest was the science of investigation.

When I began to feel as if my brain could not possibly grapple with another scientific fact or theory, Mrs. Hudson thankfully entered the apartment with a tray of tea and biscuits. That brief interruption offered

Holmes the perfect opportunity to steer the conversation to matters of his interest.

"About the incident, Professor."

"I am at a complete loss to explain. I can only tell you I was apprehended by two men and kept in seclusion for two days in a warehouse. It was most unpleasant."

"Oh, my!" Mrs. Hudson said. "How on earth did you escape?"

Holmes gave Mrs. Hudson a sharp look of disapproval.

"Begging your pardon. But it's been in the news."

"I did not escape. On the third morning of my kidnapping, I heard the door being unlocked. I waited for someone to come in, but no one did. Finally, I tried the door, it opened, and no one was there. I walked out onto the road and hailed a taxi."

"And yet you've not been to Scotland Yard?" Mrs. Hudson asked.

Any moment I expected Holmes to send Mrs. Hudson packing.

"No, I found a note fastened to the outside of the door. It said if I wanted to make sure my family was safe, now--and in the future--I should not contact the police."

"Hmm, " Holmes demurred. "*Now and in the future!* An odd phrase, wouldn't you say?"

"Is it?" Einstein asked. "I thought perhaps it was an English expression."

"If you fear for your family, why have you come to me?"

"I do not believe in giving into fear. You have a reputation, Mr. Holmes. I think you can be trusted. My sense is you can be discreet in ways the police cannot."

"Quite right."

"I had wanted very much to travel to America, and to enjoy the society of my friend H.G. Wells. I am afraid I was denied two unique opportunities."

"More tea, Professor?"

"Yes, thank you Mrs. Hudson."

As she poured a fresh cup, Mrs. Hudson took the opportunity to further her own inquiry. "You surely can book passage on another ship."

Holmes rolled his eyes. I can only think he held his tongue because Professor Einstein seemed more relaxed with Mrs. Hudson in the room.

"Of course, but I have other obligations. The trip to America was a narrow window of opportunity. I return to Germany soon. I don't know when I will have that opportunity again."

"You were not harmed by your captors?" I asked.

"Only my pride for failing to put up a meaningful defense. No, I was not mistreated. I was kept in seclusion."

Holmes rose from his chair and began to pace. His thoughts were coming fast and furiously. "As a scientist, there is surely something you observed."

"I was blindfolded."

"Something you heard. A voice? Could you recognize a voice?"

"No, my captors never spoke in my presence."

"Professor, there is always something. The sound of a walk."

Einstein thought for a moment. "Yes, the sound of a walk. There were three men, two who grabbed me from behind and blindfolded me, and another man. He walked with a slight shuffle of the foot, as if —"

"As if he had once sustained an injury or perhaps he had even used a cane!" Holmes said with such ebullience that Einstein seemed taken aback.

"I have no way of knowing."

Many individuals used canes. I couldn't imagine why Holmes thought something so common was important.

"Curious, indeed! It would seem as if the only purpose in apprehending you was to ensure that you did not board that ship for America."

"So it would seem, Mr. Holmes. But why? What possible difference could my traveling to America make to anyone? Who would have such an interest?"

"An enemy? A rival?" I said, accepting Mrs. Hudson's offer of more tea.

"I am not aware that I have any enemies, Doctor. As for rivals, at the point of sounding immodest, I have none."

That was certainly a candid admission. I suspected many in the scientific community would vehemently disagree.

"It is possible your kidnappers got cold feet, but somehow I doubt that is the case. Without more to go on, I am afraid we are at a dead-end." Holmes took a sip of tea. "One last thing, professor. The lecture you and Mr. Wells were to present. What was the subject?"

"Vermholes!"

Holmes and I looked at each other and repeated the word at the same time. "Vermholes?"

A momentary silence fell over the room.

"Wormholes!" Mrs. Hudson expostulated.

"Yes, vermholes. That is what I said," Einstein reiterated.

Having tolerated Mrs. Hudson as long as he was able, Holmes reminded her she must have more important matters to attend to.

"Thank you for reminding me. I'll leave you gentlemen to it, then. Good day, Professor."

"Thank you, Mrs. Hudson."

Mrs. Hudson exited the apartment, much to the obvious relief of Holmes.

"A very charming lady, Mr. Holmes."

"Very," Holmes replied with obvious sarcasm. "Please, go on, Professor."

"Wormholes are theoretical time tunnels between two distinct times and locations. They are like the railway tunnels that run under this glorious city. One enters at one end and comes out in a different place at a different time. But instead of traveling just a few minutes and a few miles, a wormhole would allow the traveler to enter in the present and come out somewhere else in the future. Think of it as a time portal, except rather than taking years, it takes only seconds to traverse."

All of this was a bit too much for me. "Sounds like Wells' time machine."

"Indeed. The concept of the wormhole is the inspiration for his novel *The Time Machine*. Mr. Wells and I have had many enjoyable conversations about the possibilities. Our joint lectures in America were intended to be an entertaining exploration of those possibilities. Not to put too fine a point on our presentations, but we thought it would be fun. Science can often be dreadfully dull, you know."

I sensed myself suddenly becoming a part of that camp.

"Professor, do *you* believe in wormholes?" Holmes asked.

"I believe in the theory, Mr. Holmes. Wormholes are beyond our current science to prove their existence."

"Would such a phenomenon exist only in space? Theoretically speaking."

"Theoretically speaking? No."

"Are you suggesting a wormhole could possibly exist here? Now?" I inquired.

"Dr. Watson, the same laws of physics that apply to the universe apply to our own planet."

This was simply too much. "Are you saying if all this wormhole mumbo jumbo were true, someone from the future could travel back in time to change the past?"

"Mumbo jumbo? This is a term with which I am unfamiliar."

"Malarkey." The confusion on Einstein's face was evident.

"Never mind," interjected Holmes. "To the doctor's point, is it possible someone from the future could travel back in time to change the past?"

"No, Mr. Holmes. Only the future can be altered. No one coming from the future can change what happened in this room yesterday. But any of us can change the future by influencing events today, tomorrow, and the next day."

"Professor, is travel through a wormhole possible both ways?"

"Excellent question, Doctor. So good, in fact, I will give you two answers. Yes and no. In theory one would be able to travel from the present into the future and return. But no one from the future would be able to travel backward in time."

I put down my teacup. "Why is that, professor?"

"Time moves in only one direction, forward. Think of it as a paddleball on an elastic tether. The ball springs out and then returns to its point of origin."

"I see," I said. On second thought that explanation made no sense at all.

The ever-astute Holmes correctly surmised my confusion. "Perhaps another analogy, Professor."

"Very well. Consider a stone tossed into the air. What happens to it?"

"It falls back to the earth," I answered.

"Always," Einstein concurred. "But a stone dropped from the air never returns to the air. Time proceeds in one direction only."

"Isn't what you are describing gravity?"

"Yes Doctor, but only for the purpose of analogy."

"I see," I said, pretending I was following this abstruse discussion. Instead of clarifying matters, I was becoming less certain about what I knew. "So there isn't a relationship between time and gravity?"

"Actually there is, Doctor. But I am afraid we will have to continue this conversation when we have more time." Our guest rose from his chair and offered his hand.

"More time! Quite amusing!" I chortled, rising to shake the hand of this most interesting and confusing fellow.

"In the future, perhaps I can do a better job of explaining myself. I must be going. You will let me know should you find out something about my abductors."

"Of course," Holmes replied, offering his own firm handshake. "One last thing, Professor. I wonder why Mrs. Einstein did not accompany you today?"

"She chose not to join me on this trip. She remained in Berlin.

"But, but—" I blustered.

Holmes raised his hand to stop me from going on. "Good day, Professor. Mrs. Hudson will see you out."

Einstein bid us adieu and exited the apartment.

"Holmes, what did he mean his wife remained in Germany?"

"As I suspected, the woman who came to visit us was an impostor."

"Great Scott, Holmes. An impostor? But why?"

"Yes, old chap, we were treated to a very convincing performance. Our impostor went to a great deal of trouble to make herself appear as the newspaper photographs of Mrs. Einstein. If you will recall, I said her photograph in *The Times* did not do her justice. I knew from the moment she walked into this room she was a counterfeit."

"But why the deception?"

"Indeed, Watson."

"If this woman is a friend of the Einstein's, why go to so much trouble?"

"Oh, I don't believe she is a friend." Holmes moved to the window and cast his eyes skyward, losing himself in thought.

"A deception is usually perpetrated for some sort of gain. The woman asked nothing of us except to help discover the motives behind Einstein's abduction. It doesn't make sense. It is quite the puzzle."

"Puzzle?" Holmes turned from the window, a sudden gleam appeared in his eyes. "Yes, Watson, it is that: a puzzle."

"I don't follow."

"An unassembled puzzle is merely a collection of random pieces with no obvious pattern. Once the pieces fall into place, a picture begins to emerge."

"Yes, that's the whole point of a puzzle." It was times such as these wherein Holmes proved to be his most confounding. "Let us assume someone else has glimpsed the entire picture. That person has been carefully watching us as we begin to pick through the individual pieces, unable at the moment to connect one piece to the next."

"What are the puzzle pieces, Holmes?"

"Recall our conversation in which I said I had a hunch three disparate events were somehow connected: our conversation with H.G. Wells three years ago, the unusual disappearances in Scotland, and the brief abduction of Professor Einstein."

"I think we are out on a limb here, Holmes. I grant you, someone three years ago could have observed our journey to Sandgate to meet with Wells. Why? I have no idea. But our visit with Einstein has only just concluded. The counterfeit Mrs. Einstein visited several days ago. If we allow for those occurrences, how could anyone outside of this room know what you had read in the newspaper?"

"Quite right, our trip to Sandgate could have been easily observed. Einstein was instructed not to go to the police. Recall, he came to us because he believed we could be discreet in ways the police are not. It stands to reason he would come here."

"Very well. How do you account for the newspaper articles?"

"Everyone reads *The Times*, Watson."

"But everyone does not connect three random events."

"Not everyone, Watson. Someone. How better to discover what your enemy knows than by sending an impostor to his camp?"

"Enemy? What enemy?"

"Inconclusive! Throughout our many adventures we have encountered enemies that have tested our mettle. I fear we may be facing another." A chill blew in from the window. "Let us finish our tea."

"Holmes, you perplex me. You offer up a tantalizing theory and then seemingly abandon it."

"Not abandon. At this point I can proceed no further."

"Wormholes, paddle balls, and stones dropping from the sky. It all seems a bit daffy to me."

"Our inability to prove something exists is not proof that it does not."

"Were there such a thing as a wormhole, where is it? How on earth could we possibly find it?"

"I believe I have a hunch."

"There's that word again, Holmes. Hunch! Have you any idea how exasperating you can be? The world's greatest scientist has just admitted to us he does not know whether or not a theoretical wormhole exists, but you, the world's greatest consulting detective, not only believe it to be so, you actually have an idea where it may be."

"Yes, Watson, I have a hunch. A gut feeling! My guess is whoever we are up against, either knows the location of that wormhole or they also have a hunch."

"All the more unsettling, as you are not a man prone to presentiment."

"I agree, but we are in the realm of theoretical scientific possibility. Go home Watson, freshen up, and then let us meet at King's Cross in one hour. We have a train to catch."

"Where to this time?"

"Isn't it obvious?"

"If it were obvious, I should not ask."

"I think it is time to pay another visit to H. G. Wells and his delightful wife Jane."

CHAPTER 7
Brief history of time

Two hours after departing King's Cross, Holmes and I were seated comfortably in the Wells home in Sandgate. Jane Wells offered tea and biscuits and sat with us in the comfortably appointed living room. Since our arrival, Wells himself had been anything but genial. Mrs. Wells did most of the talking, as if she had been the one on that most unfortunate trip to Scotland three years earlier.

"I am not sure what else Bertie and I can tell you, Mr. Holmes. It has been two years, after all."

"Actually it was three years ago," I added politely.

"You haven't told us everything, have you, Mr. Wells?" Holmes eyes bore into our host.

"What else is there to tell?" Mrs. Wells asked as if to rescue her husband from Holmes steely glare.

"He hasn't disclosed the location of the wormhole."

Wells shifted uncomfortably.

Jane Wells glanced at her husband. "Wormhole? What is a wormhole?"

Wells popped a biscuit into his mouth. "I have no idea what you are talking about." Crumbs sprinkled onto his tie.

"I believe you do. The theoretical possibility of a wormhole is the foundation of your novel *The Time Machine.*"

"Mr. Holmes, you surely don't believe in time travel." The notion seemed so absurd to Mrs. Wells that she chuckled. Then she felt quite embarrassed by her rudeness. She was, after all, in the company of the world's greatest detective.

"Quite right, Mrs. Wells, not as presented in your husband's novel."

"I am flattered that the great Sherlock Holmes has read my novel," Wells said with obvious satisfaction.

"I haven't read it, I have only scanned it."

"Be that as it may, I have no idea what you are driving at."

"Would you mind if I stand? I think better when I am able to move about."

The couple glanced at each other. Mrs. Wells shook her head and Mr. Wells shrugged his shoulders.

Holmes rose and began to pace. "A seemingly unrelated series of events, beginning with your curious adventure three years ago, the occasional disappearances of vagabonds in Scotland, and the kidnapping of Albert Einstein have led me to my hypothesis. Conversations with Professor Einstein and research for your novel provided you with a great deal of information into the science of wormholes. I believe your research and luck led you to the location of an actual wormhole."

"Once more. What is a wormhole?" Mrs. Wells asked.

Wells pretended amusement. "Intriguing. And if such a phenomenon were to exist, where do you think it is located?"

"Somewhere in Scotland we imagine." I answered, speaking for Holmes and myself.

"Mr. Wells, you traveled to Scotland three years ago. I shouldn't imagine it would prove too terribly difficult for Scotland Yard to reconstruct your movements."

"Scotland Yard? Are you accusing Herbert of a crime, Mr. Holmes?"

"No, Mrs. Wells, I am appealing to his sense of justice and patriotism. I am of the opinion that the most dangerous criminal mastermind this world has ever known may be in possession of the knowledge I am seeking from your husband."

"What? Moriarty?" I blurted out, spitting up my tea. This was the first I had heard of that dastardly fellow in our conversations.

"Who is Moriarty?" Jane Wells asked.

"Professor Moriarty," Holmes said.

"If that name is supposed to mean something to me, Mr. Holmes, it doesn't." Jane Wells turned to her husband. "Herbert, do you know this Professor Moriarty?"

"I believe he is a product of Dr. Watson's imagination," Wells replied.

"No doubt that is the opinion of many," Holmes said. "I suspect he goes by other names now. But I assure you he is well-known to law enforcement and, more particularly, to those who inhabit the underbelly of the criminal world."

"But, Holmes, Moriarty is dead! Like you, he went over Reichenbach Falls. It is nothing short of a miracle that you survived."

"But survive I did and so too could have Moriarty. Mr. Wells, I believe it was Moriarty who came to your home that night while you were still in Scotland. It was he who rifled through the cottage where you keep your research."

"But the proof, Holmes. The proof!"

"I have no proof, Watson. Not a shred."

I was simply flabbergasted. It was beyond comprehension that Holmes would make such assertions without a scintilla of proof.

"Mrs. Wells, you said the man had a limp and used a cane, as did I after my miraculous survival at the falls."

"Yes, that is true, that is the description. But I am still not clear who this Moriarty is. And I still have no idea what a wormhole is."

Wells broke in. "Mr. Holmes, you have a wonderful imagination. As you say, you are attempting to string together a series of seemingly unrelated events."

"That night Dr. Watson and I came to your home three years ago, there was one curiosity that intrigued me most. Mrs. Wells felt it important enough to make it a part of the notes she shared with us. One of my many interests is etymology, the study of the history and the origins of words. Mrs. Wells said you referred to the thugs who attacked you as Nazis."

"Yes," said Wells. "That is how they identified themselves."

"I have made an exhaustive study of that word and I can find no history."

For a moment Wells said nothing. It would have been clear to anyone standing in that room that his mind was racing. "All right, you have me, Mr. Holmes. It is a name I invented. I confess, I fell victim to artistic license. Call it an occupational hazard."

"I think not," Holmes said slowly and deliberately. "I am correct am I not that the reason we are unfamiliar with the term *Nazi* is because whatever or whom it refers to does not yet exist?"

Mrs. Wells turned to her husband, giving him a reproachful look. "Herbert?"

"Oh, it's Herbert now, is it?" Clearly Wells was agitated. "Yes, Mr. Holmes, it is true. That which we call a Nazi does not yet exist."

"If, as I believe, this case involves Professor Moriarty, I am most concerned. He is not a man to trifle with."

"Aren't you getting just a bit carried away, Mr. Holmes? Your choice of words has all the earmarks of cheap fiction. You paint this man as some sort of monster."

"Believe me when I tell you you should wish that is all he is. I must know how you have come to possess information that does not yet exist. Tell me about the wormhole and where I may find it."

"Bertie, Mr. Holmes is not the only one who wants to know about the wormhole. Are you going to tell us?"

"Very well." Wells rose and began to move about the room. "I prefer to call it a time portal."

"A time portal?" Jane Wells blustered. "Herbert, these gentlemen haven't traveled all this way to be insulted. Pull yourself together. Show some dignity."

Wells ignored his wife's outburst. "I have only been through it once. That was enough."

I must say I was in agreement with Mrs. Wells. This story was becoming more preposterous by the moment. Nonetheless, I felt obliged to pretend Wells' story was credible.

"How did you locate the wormhole?" Holmes inquired.

"Through painstaking research, some of Einstein's work, and a bit of good luck."

"The entrance to the portal is located in Loch Naire, is it not?" Holmes said.

Wells nodded.

"Which may well account for the disappearances that have been reported there over the years."

"Quite right, Mr. Holmes. Those disappearances became an important part of the puzzle. That anomaly was crucial to discovering the location."

Holmes never failed to amaze me. Somehow his mind had connected those random events and arrived at the same conclusion as Wells' scientific research.

"And where, pray tell, does this time portal come out?" Jane Wells asked flippantly.

"The wormhole exits in a dead-end alley in Berlin."

"Of course." Jane Wells threw up her hands. "This is the same silly story he tried to tell me three years ago."

"It comes out in the future?" Holmes asked.

"Yes, in the future." Jane Wells said in exasperation. "Eighteen years, if memory serves."

"That would make it 1936," I said.

"Three years ago, Doctor. Were one to enter the portal today, it would now be 1939."

"Eighteen years into the future." I shook my head. Wells was surely suffering from some frailty of the mind.

"Herbert, I can't imagine what has come over you. You really must take a holiday. You are speaking to Sherlock Holmes."

Holmes raised his hand. "It is quite all right, Mrs. Wells. I know this is a lot to take in. There is much about this that I don't understand. Please, Mr. Wells, don't leave off a single detail."

"As you correctly surmised, Mr. Holmes, I entered the portal in Scotland. The entry point is a few meters from the Loch Naire station. It is a site frequented by vagrants and other undesirables who board trains under the cover of darkness. Relying on a compass, the coordinates I had calculated, and the newspaper accounts, I entered a small clearing a few meters from the station and came face to face with two stones the size of houses. My intuition directed me to a crevasse between the two stones. The instant I stepped into that crevasse, I was momentarily blinded by a flash of light. A moment later, I was standing in an alley in Berlin."

CHAPTER 8
Berlin

Wells' skill as a storyteller was on fine display. As incredulous as his story sounded, I was enthralled. Whatever had happened to Wells in that instant stepping between the two stones, he apparently experienced no ill effects. That would come later at the hands of his pursuers.

The portal had deposited Wells between two buildings in a dead-end alley. It took him almost a half an hour before gathering his wits to investigate his surroundings. Daylight was beginning to wane. Steps led to various buildings. Rubbish bins overflowed with rotting food. The smell of stale beer and the noxious odors of human waste hung in the air. There were no signs that might offer a clue to his whereabouts. For all he knew, he could have been in an alley in Loch Naire. Across the way, a door opened. Light bled into the alley and polka music and laughter poured out. A stout fellow wearing an apron tossed a bucket of water into the alley and then went back inside, kicking the door closed behind him. Wells had stayed well out of sight. Now he had a clue. The polka music and laughter meant he was probably in an alley behind a pub. All right, he thought to himself, I'll investigate. But first he needed to get his bearings. He needed to fix the precise spot in his mind where the portal had deposited him. Where the two buildings met, there was a small recess as if perhaps a walk through had been there once, but was now filled in. The recess was deep enough for a man to stand in unobserved; otherwise it served no obvious purpose. Wells took a deep breath and walked out of the alley and onto the street. There wasn't anything familiar or remarkable about the street, except for the fact that all of the shop and street signs were written in German. Wells considered re-entering the portal, but curiosity got the better of him. If he were in Germany, where precisely, and more importantly, when? He walked to the end of the block and rounded the corner in search of the tavern. Two doors down a sign swung above an entrance that read *Eisen John*. Iron John. "Manly," Wells thought to himself. "Hopefully pleasant." Wells straightened his tie and entered the tavern. At first glance the tavern looked like any one might find in England. It was filled with revelers, music, and conversation. On closer inspection, Wells realized most of the patrons were uniformed soldiers. At once the entire establishment went deathly quiet. As Wells approached the bar, two soldiers stepped in front of him.

"Wer bist du?" said one of the soldiers.

"Excuse me?"

"Ein Engländer hier?" The second soldier seemed to ask incredulously.

Wells wasn't exactly fluent in German, but he was able to sort out enough to discern the presence of an Englishman in a German tavern was out of the ordinary. He glanced around to see if there were any patrons in the tavern that weren't soldiers. There was only a handful. Wells noted the men's suits were quite different from the one he was wearing. They seemed somehow more modern. Had he traveled forward in time?

"I'm not sure if you chaps read science fiction, but I am H. G. Wells the science fiction writer."

The second soldier seemed quite upset that an Englishman had come into his tavern. "Ein Englander hier in Berlin?"

That answered one part of the puzzle. "Berlin? Oh, is that where I am?"

The two soldiers folded their arms in front of them and glanced at each other, as if to suggest a plan of action was needed to deal with this interloper. Wells quickly deduced he wasn't welcome, nor should he stay, but he could not leave without discovering the date. He could desperately use a drink to bolster his resolve. His eyes wandered to the bar behind the two soldiers standing in front of him. He wondered if he might get a good Irish or Scotch whisky. On the wall behind the bar, something caught his attention. It was a photograph of a funny little fellow with a tiny moustache under his nose. He was holding up a hand as if swearing an oath. Wells wondered if this chap was the German counterpart of Charlie Chaplin. Then something more important caught his eye. Below the picture was a calendar. The year read 1936. Wells froze. Could it be true? Had he really traveled eighteen years into the future? The expired days on the calendar were marked with an X. The last mark was through Tuesday, which meant today was Wednesday, the same day he had entered the portal. The month was the same, yet something seemed amiss, something wasn't adding up.

The soldier who had been doing all the talking leaned uncomfortably close, interrupting Wells' train of thought. "Was machst du hier?"

"Just passing through," Wells said, guessing he had answered the soldier's question. "Say, who are you chaps, anyway?"

In unison both soldiers said as a matter of obvious pride, "Wir sind Nazis!"

Wells had never heard of a Nazi before. As he attempted to sort out what a Nazi might be, one of the soldiers reached for the holster hanging beneath his arm. Unarmed and not especially given to heroics, Wells reacted instinctively. He lunged forward, pushed the soldier reaching for his pistol into his companion and fled like a mad man for the door. That split second of disorientation undoubtedly saved his life. As he disappeared through the tavern entrance, a shot fired off behind him. The bullet grazed Wells' calf. It was as if a red-hot poker had been pressed against his leg. The pain was unbearable, but he didn't have a second to lose. If he didn't get to the portal, he couldn't imagine what might be in store for him.

The Nazis gave chase, but those few seconds of head start had given Wells just enough time to re-enter the portal. As for the Nazis, they were at a complete loss to explain how they had lost this man. A thorough search of the alley revealed nothing. The man had simply disappeared in a dead-end alley. Should they report the incident to their superiors? They would think on that for a while. If this man were a spy and they had let him escape, there were methods and ways to deal with those who failed in their duty. The incident would go unreported.

An instant later Wells found himself once again in the clearing in front of the two gigantic stones. His wound was nasty and bleeding profusely, but it was not life threatening. It would be a long, uncomfortable journey home. Wells had had his fill of portals and Scotland. He desperately needed the comforts of home and a loving wife.

CHAPTER 9
Eliminating the impossible

After hearing Wells' story, Holmes didn't mince words. "I must have the location of the wormhole."

Wells seemed hesitant, but Holmes was insistent.

"Herbert, I think you must," Jane Wells said. "If Mr. Holmes believes it is important, then you must cooperate."

"Yes, of course." Wells went to the bureau and took out pen and paper. "I shall write out everything you need to know."

"One last thing, does Professor Einstein know about your discovery?"

"No, I haven't told him."

"After three years, that's quite extraordinary," I felt compelled to point out.

"Dr. Watson, I hope you can fully appreciate how traumatic my experience was. I am fully aware of the scientific and historic importance of my discovery."

"Then why have you kept it to yourself?" I asked.

"I haven't fully come to terms with who should know and how my discovery should be announced. I fear that knowledge in the wrong hands could have far reaching consequences."

"I quite agree. Which is precisely the reason Dr. Watson and I have a train to catch. You have been most helpful."

Jane Wells perked up. "The least we can do is to drive you to the station. I'll drive. Bertie can talk."

Minutes later we were in the Wells' sedan on our way out of Sandgate headed toward Folkestone Central Station. Jane Wells proved a more than capable driver.

"I am very upset at you, Bertie. You lied to me. You said a gang of thugs in Scotland beat you up."

The speed of the car seemed to be increasing with the rising intensity of Jane Wells' anger. Holmes and I each reached for a safety strap.

"I tried to tell you the truth, but you wouldn't believe me."

"It was such a preposterous story."

I felt I needed to intervene. We were going uncomfortably fast. "Even if this preposterous story is true—"

"It is true, Doctor," Wells said defensively.

"If, as Holmes surmises, Professor Moriarty is involved—"

"I assure you he is, old chap. Every bone in my body tells me so." Holmes leaned forward to glance into the rearview mirror.

"Who is Moriarty again?" Jane Wells asked, looking over her shoulder.

"Please pay attention to the road, darling." Wells reached for the steering wheel.

"He is a criminal mastermind," I replied.

"This is the man with the limp?"

"Yes." Wells wiped his forehead. The implications of what he had been involved in were becoming clearer by the moment.

"You think this Moriarty chap is up to something nefarious?" Jane Wells asked.

"Without question, Mrs. Wells." I added. "Many regard him as the Napoleon of Crime."

"That's a silly sounding name: The Napoleon of Crime. I should be embarrassed to be known by a name like that. Am I right?"

"Always," her husband said.

"Whether the name fits or not, it goes without saying the man is always up to something."

"But what?"

"We have no way of knowing until we confront him," Holmes said.

"How will you find him, Mr. Holmes?"

That was the rub, wasn't it? If Moriarty really were alive, he could be anywhere. I mean no pun when I say he literally dropped out of sight. Holmes himself said the last glimpse he ever had of the man was seconds before he disappeared into the roiling waters of the falls. Holmes himself was spared death by the sheer force of the water. Having plunged unaccountably deep below the surface of the water, a burst of kinetic energy shot a massive volume of water upward, shooting Holmes to the surface and smashing him onto a rock. His body broken, he lay unconscious for hours on that rock, miraculously out of the way of further harm. What happened after has never been made public. As much as it grieved me then, it grieves me now that my trusted friend never shared with me how he was rescued and by whom. For three long years I lived with the belief that Sherlock Holmes had died at Reichenbach. That Moriarty may have also survived and has been in seclusion since is beyond my ability to fathom. How had he survived? How had he been rescued? Where has he been? Clearly Holmes had considered the possibility of Moriarty's survival long before sharing his thoughts with me. I was as eager as Jane Wells for an answer to her question.

"Excellent question, Mrs. Wells. I have spent a fair amount of time considering where the world's most dangerous criminal would feel safest."

"What have you come up with, Holmes?" Enough of this dilly-dallying. I had spent entirely too long being kept in the dark about Reichenbach.

"There is only one possibility. I am sure Mr. Wells has already considered that possibility."

Wells knew exactly where Holmes was going. "Where else, but in the future."

"What?" I ejaculated.

"Other than death, how else to explain Moriarty's virtual disappearance from existence?"

"Bertie, you are so clever." Jane Wells clapped her hands.

"Thank you, darling. Hands on the wheel please!"

At this point, I might have believed Holmes himself had been hiding out in the future all those years were it not for the fact that he had practically threatened Wells to provide him with a map to the location of the portal.

Jane Wells put her hands back on the steering wheel. "One thing I don't understand—"

"One?" Holmes, Wells, and I said at the same time.

"Professor Moriarty came looking for Herbert because he was convinced Herbert had discovered the wormhole. But what did that have to do with Professor Einstein?"

Wells considered his wife's question. "The wormhole comes out in Germany. Einstein is German."

"Which means what?" Jane Wells asked.

For several moments the only sound was that of the car racing toward the station. I studied the face of my good friend and colleague. I knew the wheels and cogs must be whirring rapidly. And then Holmes finally spoke.

"What if Moriarty discovered something in the future that he could change by coming back to the present?"

"Is such a thing possible?" I asked.

"Theoretically it is possible as long as the event has not already happened in the present," Wells responded.

Holmes continued. "What if Moriarty is the catalyst for a change in events and Einstein is the key?"

"I shudder to think," Wells offered. "As we do not know nor can we predict the future, we are at the mercy of a time traveller who could possibly change the course of events before they can happen. As a novelist, I cannot help but think there are hundreds of possibilities, perhaps thousands of outcomes."

"It is most worrisome," Holmes said with uncharacteristic apprehension.

"Here we are." Jane Wells brought the car to a quick stop in front of the Folkestone Central Station.

As the car sat idling in front of the station entrance, another car came to a halt several meters away. Its lights extinguished, but the occupants did not exit the vehicle.

"Thank you both," Holmes said. "You have been most congenial and helpful."

Holmes and I stepped into the crisp night air.

Wells joined us outside and offered his hand. "One last thing, Mr. Holmes. Shouldn't finding Moriarty be like searching for a needle in a haystack?"

Holmes glanced toward the car that had pulled in to the station car park but whose occupants had not gotten out. "If Moriarty has a single weakness, it is that he has a compulsive need to keep an eye on Dr. Watson and me. Finding him is simply a matter of Moriarty finding us."

H.G. Wells held out a firm hand. "I wish you success."

"Good luck to you both, Mr. Holmes." Jane Wells placed her delicate hand in mine and then in Holmes' hand.

"Thank you, Mrs. Wells. Ordinarily I don't invoke the need for luck, but in this instance, I believe we may well need it."

CHAPTER 10
Train to Scotland

After expressing our gratitude to Wells and his wife for their hospitality, Holmes and I boarded the train for our return trip to King's Cross Station. At times such as these Holmes was reticent, his mind racing ahead, enumerating the possibilities that the future held. I busied myself with the day's paper. When Holmes was ready to share his thoughts, he would let me know.

The trip to King's Cross took approximately two hours. Our day had been long and tiring. We needed a good night's rest before embarking on the next phase of our journey. Upon arrival at King's Cross, Holmes insisted I spend the night at Baker Street. Of course I was no stranger to Baker Street. That is, after all, where Holmes and I shared the more than adequate quarters of 221 B for many years prior to my meeting and marrying Mary Morstand, the late Mrs. Watson. Upon our nuptials, Mrs. Watson and I occupied a residence in Paddington. I do believe those years apart were difficult for Holmes, although he would never admit that he had preferred my company to solitude. After the passing of Mrs. Watson, Holmes invited me to return to 221 B. I accepted his gracious offer and for a time I reacquainted myself with Baker Street. With Holmes as my companion once again, his society helped fill the emptiness of life without Mary. I remained with Holmes for several months. In time my despair waned and I felt it was time to face life once again. I had always valued Holmes' friendship and would continue to do so; however, unlike my friend, I was not a solitary man. And so I took up residence in Belgravia. Upon the recommendation of Mrs. Hudson, I engaged the services of a Mrs. Portland, an acquaintance, and, like

Mrs. Hudson, a widow herself. Mrs. Portland proved most agreeable. She comported herself in the most excellent manner and in no time I wondered how I had gotten along without her. I thanked Mrs. Hudson for introducing us. As for Holmes, whatever disappointment he felt upon my leaving, he kept to himself, but I knew him well enough to know he would have preferred my remaining at Baker Street. As we continued to work together on cases, I was at Baker Street so often it was as if I had not really left.

After our visit to Sandgate, I could easily have returned to my home in Belgravia, but Holmes seemed keen on my staying over at Baker Street. I accepted his offer and spent the night in my old room, left exactly the way it had been on my final day there. I should have slept comfortably, but my rest was fitful. My thoughts were positively overwhelmed with the events of the day and what the future had in store.

At seven o'clock the following morning Euston Station was already teeming with activity. Trains were shunting in and out of the station. Passengers and porters crowded the platforms. Goods of every description were being loaded and unloaded for travel to and from every part of England. One doesn't fully appreciate the richness and diversity of London life until one visits one of its many stations.

After exiting our taxi we boarded The Royal Scot for Edinburg. Our point of termination would occur at the coal and water stop of Loch Naire. By my calculations we had a good five hours of travel time ahead of us.

The effects of a poor night's sleep left me tired and sluggish. As our journey got underway, I found myself dozing on and off. Occasionally other passengers would pass by our compartment and out of natural habit glance through the glass. I paid no attention, but of course Holmes was ever alert. I had long been used to Holmes' remarkable powers of observation; the sheer volume of information he could take in never ceased to amaze me.

Well into our journey, Holmes tapped his foot against mine. "I say, Watson, all this rushing about has given me a devil of an appetite."

Mrs. Hudson had offered to serve breakfast, but the departure time hadn't allowed for a morning meal.

"I believe I shall go to the dining car. Care to join me?"

"No, old boy, you go on. I can't seem to come awake."

"Right, then." Holmes rose and slid open the door of the compartment and exited in the direction of the dining car.

"Fancy that," I mumbled to myself. Holmes had forgotten his hat. It was still lying on the seat. I reached across the aisle to the opposite seat and retrieved the hat. Perhaps I would take it to him. Getting up and having a walk might perk me up, in addition to having a cup of coffee.

As I contemplated the hat, the compartment door slid open.

"Hello?" I said, before actually looking up to see who had entered the compartment.

A rather striking woman dressed in black stood in front of the door. She reached behind her back and slid the door closed. I rose to introduce myself.

"Are you Sherlock Holmes?" The woman asked, speaking in an accent I couldn't quite place.

Before I had the chance to say a word, the woman threw herself into my arms.

"Mr. Holmes, I need your help."

"What? Yes, er—"

65

"Thank goodness, you've got to help me. Some men are after me."

"Men? What men?" I said, suddenly aware that I was embracing a complete stranger rather intimately.

"Oh, I don't know. Men. Sinister men. Horrible men. Spies. Secret agents. Who knows?"

"But why? What do they want of you?"

"Maybe something to do with my boyfriend."

"Your boyfriend? What has he done?" Suddenly I felt rather compromised in the arms of another man's companion.

"Maybe he stole some secrets. Oh, you've got to help me Mr. Holmes."

"Secrets? What secrets?"

At that moment the train entered the first of several tunnels. The sound of the train became more intense and the compartment was engulfed in darkness.

"What is going on?" The woman in my arms cried.

"It's just a tunnel. We'll be out soon."

The train roared once again into daylight.

"See, you're safe."

"You've got to protect me. Say you'll protect me."

"Of course I will, but I don't even know your name, Miss—"

"Francois."

"Pleased to meet you, Miss Francois."

"Please, call me Francoise."

"All right, Francoise."

At that moment the compartment door slid open and Holmes stepped inside.

"Holmes!"

"Watson!"

The woman in my arms pushed me away. "What? You're not Sherlock Holmes? Get your hands off me, you imposter." She slapped my face.

"I never said—"

"Sherlock Holmes at your service. How do you do? I see you have already met my colleague Dr. Watson."

"Holmes, this is not what it seems," I said rising from the seat I had been pushed onto by the woman in black.

"It is quite all right, old fellow. I see how it is, an innocent case of mistaken identity."

"Well, yes, I can see how one might be confused." In truth, I rather enjoyed that momentary mistake. "Holmes, this is Miss Francois."

"Call me, Francoise."

"Yes--anyway—Miss Francoise Francois is in some sort of trouble. She needs our protection."

"What man can resist a damsel in distress?"

"Thank you," the woman replied. "You are most kind, Mr. Holmes."

"I am surprised you do not recognize this woman, Watson. She is the same woman who pretended to be Mrs. Einstein."

"What?" How was that possible? The two women looked nothing alike.

"Watson, allow me to introduce Vera Erikson, a colleague of Professor Moriarty."

Immediately the mystery woman who Holmes called Vera Erikson pulled a pistol from her purse.

"Surprised, Miss Erikson? You shouldn't be. My network of associates was able to identify you within a matter of hours after your visit as Mrs. Einstein."

"Sit down, Mr. Holmes." Vera Erikson used the pistol as a pointer. "Across from Dr. Watson." Then she turned the pistol toward me. "You sit as well, Doctor." I did as I was told. "You are very clever, Mr. Holmes. I thought my impersonation of Mrs. Einstein was rather good."

"What purpose was served by the theatrics?"

"Information, Doctor. It was necessary to learn what you and Mr. Holmes had discovered."

"Up until the point you appeared, I am not sure we had discovered much of anything. We had nothing concrete to go on."

"The doctor is right. Professor Moriarty may have gotten a little anxious. I think he may have overplayed his hand."

Vera Erikson moved the pistol back and forth between Holmes and myself. "I don't understand."

"It is like putting the cart before the horse," I added as a point of clarification.

"Horses and hands! I don't understand what you are saying!"

"Simply that the Professor assumed we knew more than we actually knew at the time you appeared. That you haven't even bothered to disabuse us of the notion that Moriarty is involved more than confirms our worst suspicions. Whenever the Professor has something new planned, his surveillance of me is always increased."

"You realize I cannot possibly allow you to continue your journey."

"Naturally, but you have made one minor miscalculation."

"Oh? And what is that?"

At that instant the train sped into another tunnel. The entire compartment went black. In the dark there were grunts and groans, pushing and shoving, none of it very gentlemanly to be sure.

When the train sped back into daylight, the scene was quite different. Holmes was standing with the pistol in the very spot where Vera Erikson had been standing. Now she was seated where Holmes had been sitting.

"Well, it seems the tables have turned. Good show, Holmes."

"Thank you, Watson. Now Miss Erikson, you are going to tell us Professor Moriarty's plan. What is his interest in the wormhole?"

"I cannot tell you anything. He would have me killed."

"If you don't tell us what we want to know, we shall throw you from the train." Keeping the pistol carefully trained on Miss Erikson, Holmes went to the window and raised it with his free hand. The wind roared as the train sped toward Scotland.

"The great Sherlock Holmes threatening a defenseless woman? Not your style Mr. Holmes." Vera Erikson moved to the window and slammed it closed.

"Hardly defenseless. But quite right, we do have other means—"

Before Holmes could finish his thought, the train entered another tunnel and once more we were plunged into darkness. Another scuffle ensued. It was impossible to have any sense of what was going on. When daylight reappeared, Holmes and I had switched places and I was the one with the pistol.

"My compliments, doctor. I underestimated you."

"Don't be ridiculous. Holmes and I are colleagues. I've saved his life--before."

"I beg you to be cautious, Miss Erikson," Holmes said. "This is not going to end well for you."

"On the contrary."

Yet another tunnel plunged us into darkness once again. Someone twisted my wrist and wrested the pistol away from me. I threw a punch but only hit air. "Holmes," I cried.

"Watson!"

Daylight flooded the compartment once again. This time Vera Erikson had the pistol pointed at us both. "This is going to end very badly for you and Dr. Watson. Say your goodbyes, gentlemen."

I hated to agree with her, but I felt she was right. It didn't look as if Holmes and I had a way out. Then miraculously the train roared into another tunnel. Holmes leapt to his feet and shoved Vera Erikson hard against the door. It was a brutish thing to do, but Vera Erikson wasn't being very ladylike in attempting to dispatch us with her pistol. The instant her head cracked hard against the glass, a shot rang out sending a bolt of blue flame from the barrel of her pistol. Glass shattered behind us and immediately the roar of the wind, the hiss of steam, and the clatter of rails were deafening. "To the roof, Watson!" I suspected Vera Erikson was out cold.

"Is that prudent?" I yelled above the deafening noise.

"There are others, Watson. We have no choice."

As our compartment was the last one in our carriage, a crude metal ladder ran up the side of the window to the roof. Such ladders were installed to allow railroad personnel access to the roof so they could check for damage and inspect the air vents on top of the carriages. Holmes and I scrambled through the window, up the ladder and onto the roof of the speeding train. Had I had time to think on what we were about to do, I might have reconsidered, but in a moment of crisis one doesn't have the luxury of being able to consider all the possibilities of what might go wrong.

"Brilliant, Holmes. Absolutely brilliant." I dared not look down.

"Not so fast, Watson. I am afraid we are not out of the woods yet."

And the end of the next carriage, two men scrambled onto the roof, making their way unsteadily toward us.

Holmes screamed above the noise of the train. "Moriarty's men. I observed them earlier while you were dozing off."

We had no choice but to fight. Under normal circumstances the men would have attacked with the ferocity of tigers, but the wind was so strong, it was as if we were throwing punches underwater. Any observer standing on the ground would have seen a slow motion ballet atop a speeding train. Holmes and I did our best to fend off our attackers, but they were younger and stronger. It occurred to me this could well be the end for Holmes and me. The train rounded a bend, momentarily throwing each of us off balance. Holmes took advantage and lunged at both men, pushing them back far enough to allow us a few valuable seconds.

"Run, Watson!" Holmes disappeared behind me, dashing toward the front of the train.

"Where to?" I cried, having exchanged places with my pursuers.

"The dining car." I could barely hear Holmes above the rush of the wind and the sudden blast of the whistle.

"What?" I said, turning

"Duck, Watson."

"I hate duck! Gives me indigestion!"

"Tunnel, Watson. Duck!"

An image flashed into my mind. Instantly I dove to the roof of the carriage. I had blocked the view of the oncoming tunnel rushing toward us just long enough so that our pursuers had no time to react. I closed my eyes. There was a horrible thud and grunt the instant the train tore into the tunnel. When we emerged into daylight again, Holmes and I were the only ones left on the roof.

We climbed down the ladder to the dining car and entered, looking windblown, but otherwise no worse for wear. We arrived too late for breakfast and too early for lunch, so we ordered something called brunch. Croissants, fresh fruit, and an ample pot of coffee were much-needed restoratives.

"Do you think we are safe here?" I asked, sipping a rather strong cup of coffee that I gripped with both hands.

"For the time being. I am afraid Miss Erikson will not be in any condition to bother us further."

"Holmes, I owe you an apology. You were right all along. Moriarty."

"No, no apology necessary. I don't believe either of us imagined Moriarty would also have survived Reichenbach."

"But how did you know?"

"I didn't know, Watson. It was our conversations with Einstein and Wells that brought into focus those hazy ideas that were beginning to take shape. They led me to consider that I had been too quick to regard the inconceivable as impossible. Twenty-four hours ago had you told me Moriarty was still alive, I would have said, impossible. Had you told me of the existence of a wormhole, I would also have said, impossible. We are easily deceived by the comforts of our prejudices."

"I am not sure Einstein is convinced the wormhole exists."

"When Mr. Wells told us he had kept one of the world's greatest discoveries secret for fear that knowledge might fall into the wrong hands, I cast all doubts aside. I had to act on my feelings, Watson, not the facts."

The steam whistle sounded.

"We are slowing down." I said.

"A brief stop. Two more stops lie ahead before we reach Loch Naire. It will be at that last stop where Moriarty will make his move. He cannot afford to allow us to get to Loch Naire. We will disembark at the next stop."

For well over half an hour, the conductor interrogated Holmes and me. He was at a complete loss to understand how we had managed to break a window in our compartment. Holmes concocted a story that he had fallen against it when the train had entered a sharp bend. Restitution would be required the conductor said. Holmes handed the man one of his cards. If the conductor had ever heard of Sherlock Holmes, he did not acknowledge that fact. He was only concerned with an address the railway company could send a bill for damages.

CHAPTER 11
Moriarty

When Vera Erikson exited the train at the next stop, Moriarty was waiting. He listened impatiently while Miss Erikson recounted the events on the train and the horrible incident atop the train that had eliminated two of his henchmen. Moriarty did not like failure.

"It wasn't my fault," Miss Erikson said in defense of herself.

"You were supposed to shoot them."

"It was the tunnels."

"Excuses. I hate excuses and I despise incompetence even more. You let Sherlock Holmes outsmart you."

"He's Sherlock Holmes. You're the one who brags that the only man in the world as smart as you is Sherlock Holmes. I don't understand why you didn't let me kill him that day you sent me to Baker Street in that ridiculous disguise."

"Do you really imagine you could have shot Sherlock Holmes in his own apartment in broad daylight on a busy London street? By the time Scotland Yard finished with you, you would have been singing like a canary. It was essential to discover what Sherlock Holmes knew."

"He didn't know much of anything, did he? So it didn't matter much."

"Sherlock Holmes has a very powerful brother in the upper echelon of the British government. That Holmes had not discussed Einstein's disappearance with his brother is critical. It is enough that Holmes himself has now gotten wind of the wormhole. Should that knowledge find its way to Whitehall, our plans will be imperiled."

The train whistled. It was time to depart.

"Should I get on?"

"No, it is no longer safe for you to be on board. We must get ahead of the train. We will continue by car."

The train whistled again and began slowly shunting from the station. A large cloud of white steam blew across the platform like a thick fog.

"Won't Holmes be expecting us to make our move in Loch Naire?"

"Of course, which is why he and Dr. Watson will disembark at Glen Donich, the last stop before Loch Naire."

"And we will be there to meet them," Vera Erikson said with a smile of satisfaction. She gently rubbed the lump on the back of her head. "I have a score to settle with Mr. Holmes."

Moriarty and Vera Erikson exited the station through the waiting room to a parked car outside.

As the large cloud of steam discharged by The Royal Scot dissipated, Holmes and I appeared to magically materialize on the station platform.

"Holmes, are you sure Moriarty will make his move at Glen Donich?"

"I think he must. It is too much of a risk allowing us to make it all the way to Loch Naire. Should we discover the entrance to the wormhole, there are simply too many variables to control for if something does not go as planned."

"All well and good, but we are without transportation. We can't hope to catch up to Moriarty now."

"I chose this village for a reason, Watson. There is a small aerodrome nearby. We shall hire a plane and fly the rest of the way."

When The Royal Scot shunted into Glen Donich, Moriarty and Vera Erikson were waiting. On the other side of the rails, two henchmen waited in case Holmes and I tried to exit the opposite side of the train. For more than a quarter of an hour after The Royal Scot had departed, Moriarty and company waited patiently until the obvious became clear. Holmes and I were not on the train.

CHAPTER 12
The Wormhole

Holmes and I arrived in Loch Naire well ahead of schedule. We quickly paid the chap who had flown us on ahead and made our way to the station. The Royal Scot wasn't due for another hour and Moriarty would be almost another hour behind the train. We quickly made our way to the station. We did not immediately enter. Holmes suggested we stay hidden until we had had a chance to survey the scene and were satisfied no suspicious characters were pretending to be waiting passengers or disinterested parties. Once assured all was clear, Holmes and I stepped onto the platform. For the next quarter of an hour Holmes and I sat patiently on a bench outside the waiting room, keeping an eye out for anyone who might look suspicious. Passengers and workers were slowly beginning to assemble for the arrival of The Royal Scot. Occasionally someone would catch my eye and I would nudge Holmes with my elbow. He would stare a few seconds and then shake his head. Holmes was brilliant that way. He could stare into a crowd and pick out the one who was trying to look inconspicuous.

"How can you be sure, Holmes?"

"It is a lot like a high stakes card game, old chap. The idea is to bluff, to avoid giving away your hand, but invariably bluffers always have a tell."

"A tell?" I asked.

"Yes. It is usually a tic or a mannerism that invariably gives one away. The more casual and relaxed one tries to appear, the stiffer they actually become, as if an automaton."

"And you see no one here that fits the bill?"

"There are plenty of people on this platform with secrets and agendas, but none who are interested in us. We are safe for the time being."

Holmes reached into a pocket and removed a compass and the meticulously hand drawn map provided by Wells. He snapped open the silver case and held the compass in his upturned hand. He rotated the small device until it registered true north. "This way, Watson."

We made our way to the far end of the platform. There sat one solitary bench. It seemed unlikely anyone other than the engineer or the coal crew would avail themselves of the comforts of that bench. Steps descended from the platform to the level of the rails. A few meters further on lay a thicket. Holmes pushed in as if he were familiar with the surroundings. I followed Holmes into the thicket, which unexpectedly opened into a small clearing. As Wells had described, there were The Stones, two mammoth outcroppings of stone resting side by side.

"This is it, Watson," Holmes said with that familiar cadence of excitement in his voice.

"Where is the entrance?" I asked.

"Between these two stones."

"But it is hardly deep enough for a man to stand in."

"We will take Wells at his word."

"Are you going in now?"

"I think I must. You remain here. Keep a lookout."

At once I was overcome with second thoughts. What I had gradually allowed myself to become less skeptical of now seemed patently absurd. Clearly Wells was having us on. Undoubtedly we were the objects of an elaborate joke. Holmes would attempt to press himself into the crevasse between the stones and nothing would happen. He would be standing there looking silly, imagining that any moment he would suddenly disappear. I would look even sillier expecting the impossible to happen. To anyone looking on, we would appear as a pair of silly old fools making asses of ourselves.

"All right, Watson, I am ready." Holmes pressed himself into the space between the two stones. I glanced away, feeling terribly embarrassed for both of us should someone be looking on.

In that brief moment my gaze turned from Holmes, there was a flash like lightning and a whooshing sound. I returned my gaze to the two stones. Holmes was gone.

"Holmes? Holmes?" I repeated several times. There was no answer. The crevasse between the two stones was empty. Sherlock Holmes had vanished.

I recalled Holmes frequent admonition that once we rule out the impossible, we are then forced to consider the improbable. My rational mind once again mulled my previous thought that I was the victim of an elaborate prank. I scoured the small clearing, thinking Holmes would pop out of the thicket and pronounce that the joke was on me, that he had just pulled off a magic trick for which there was an easy explanation. I waited several minutes anticipating that Holmes would magically reappear until it became apparent some explanation other than a prank was at work here. The small clearing offered nothing in the way of comfort, so I made my way back to the station, climbed the steps and sat on the solitary bench at the end of the platform. I opened my pocket watch and noted the time. It was impossible to say how long Holmes would be gone.

During Holmes' absence The Royal Scot arrived, loaded and unloaded passengers, took on water and coal, and continued on its way to Edinburgh. I held my breath hoping that neither Moriarty nor his companions might disembark. As Holmes calculated, the Professor would not arrive for another hour.

Shortly after The Royal Scot left the station, a scruffy looking vagrant with a knapsack tied to the end of a stick that he carried over his shoulder came down the railway line from the direction the train had departed. He ascended the steps and sat next to me on the bench.

"What you doing then?" The vagrant asked me.

"I am waiting for a friend," I replied.

"I don't suppose you have any loose change you can spare, do you, guvnor?"

"I don't carry spare change," I bristled. "And please don't refer to me as guvnor."

"You a copper then?"

"No, I am a doctor."

"What you doing here then?"

"Mind your own business, you impertinent fellow."

"I'm making it my business. This is my bench."

"Don't be ridiculous. This bench belongs to the station."

"It's mine until someone says otherwise. Now what you really doing here?"

"I told you, I am waiting for a friend."

"A gentleman like you in a place like this?"

Would this man not leave me alone? He had gone beyond irritant. Now he was a nuisance. "Very well, I'm on a case. It's top secret."

"Oh, really? Top secret, eh? So you are a copper. What's stopping me from conking you on the head and taking your money?"

Good lord. This fellow was becoming unbearable. "I have a pistol in my pocket!"

"Show it to me."

"I will not."

"Then you don't have one."

"I do. Don't come closer or I'll shoot." I said rising from the bench, as if standing over the man would make me seem more threatening.

"That's just your finger in your pocket."

"'Tis not. I'll shoot, stand back. I mean it."

"I dare you."

"What makes you think I don't have a pistol?"

"A well-dressed gentleman like you wouldn't shoot a hole through a lovely overcoat like that. You'd pull out the pistol and just pop off a few shots."

"Assuming I don't have a pistol, what do you want?"

"How about a pound?"

"Great Scott! That's absolute robbery."

"Well, yes, that's the whole point of robbery."

"Very well." I slapped a pound note into this bothersome man's hand. "Now, be off."

"My bench," the vagrant said. "I'm not going anywhere."

I resigned myself to sharing the bench with this most irksome fellow. For some while I found myself wondering who would show up first, Moriarty or Holmes. Finally, I could keep my eyes open no longer. As I was about to nod off, the vagrant elbowed me in the ribs. "Who's this coming then?"

"What?" I said, snapping awake.

"Him!" The vagrant pointed in the direction of the thicket.

Immediately I felt a flood of relief. "It's my friend, Sherlock Holmes."

"Right, and I am Dr. Watson."

"What? *I'm* Dr. Watson. I say, Holmes, this man has been a proper nuisance. Won't leave me alone."

"Never mind, Watson. Quick, give me a pound."

"What?"

"A pound note, quickly."

I handed a pound note to Holmes. Immediately he shoved it into the hand of the vagrant. "Here, take this. You have been most helpful."

"He hasn't done anything!" I blurted out, completely aghast.

"He can do something now. If anyone asks, you haven't seen us. Got that?"

The vagrant looked at the two crisp pound notes in his hand. "I've not seen a thing."

"Good, now wait at the entrance to the station."

"As you wish, guvnor."

Holmes waited patiently as the vagrant entered the station. "It is as Wells said, Watson. The world has changed. Only much worse than he could have imagined."

"Changed how?"

"Gone mad. Germany has been taken over by a madman."

"Moriarty has taken control of Germany?"

"No, my friend, a fellow named Adolph Hitler. He is far more dangerous than Moriarty. I had so little time, but from what little I learned, I believe this Hitler poses a threat to the entire free world. A war unlike anything we can imagine may be looming."

"But how? We have just come through a war. Germany was utterly defeated. The country is in ruin. The articles of surrender would never allow for such a thing."

"Yes, today, now, here. But I am speaking of Germany in 1939. That war you speak of ended twenty-years ago. Under Hitler's leadership, a new Germany is building a formidable war machine and already preying upon weaker nations. If he is not stopped, I shudder to think what may happen."

"What are you saying, Holmes? Have you a plan to do away with this Hitler chap?"

"No, that would be quite impossible. He is well insulated. An assassin could never get close enough. England and her allies are in great danger. This man is bent on world domination. I am afraid, the rest of the world has underestimated him."

"How did you manage to find out so much in a short time? You must know a little German."

"In a manner of speaking, yes. I met a rather small but well built German chap after I went through. He has studied at Cambridge, quite fluent in English. He had much to share. I think we must return to the portal immediately."

"We?"

"Yes, we have much to do."

"But Holmes, the day is almost over. You must be exhausted. I know I am. We've not dined nor rested. Is it advisable to make another journey with so little sustenance and rest?"

"Quite right, my friend. I have made arrangements for us to stay in a small hotel not far from the portal. I am completely confident we will be safe."

"I could never pass myself off as German."

"That is why you must be quiet and let me do the talking. Come."

Reluctantly I followed Holmes through the thicket and into the clearing. Once again we stood before the two monoliths that would transport us to the future. Holmes sensed my apprehension. Before I could object, Holmes pushed me into the crevasse.

Moriarty paced the platform at Glen Donich. Vera Erikson sat on a bench with her legs crossed, absentmindedly twirling her foot in such a way that it would slide in and out of her shoe.

A pair of Moriarty's henchmen approached.

"Well?"

"Nothing. We've searched everywhere. Holmes and Watson are not on the train."

"Then they disembarked at the same stop as we did."

Vera Erikson took out a nail file and began filing her nails. "Whole lot of good that did us. It seems Sherlock Holmes has outwitted you."

"He did not outwit me. He merely pulled a fast one."

"I am sure I can't appreciate the difference."

"Here's something you may appreciate, my dear. Life is short. Enjoy it while you can."

Clearly Sherlock Holmes had gotten under Moriarty's skin. It wouldn't do for Vera Erikson to add to Moriarty's irritation. She thought better of making any more comments, at least for the time being.

"By now Holmes will have reached the portal. We have no choice. We must press on to Berlin."

"Oh, no, not tonight," Vera Erikson protested. "I need a bath, a good dinner, and a good night's rest."

Moriarty looked at his watch. By the time he and Vera Erikson arrived at the portal, it would be too late to accomplish much. He would have to depend on his contacts in Berlin. Unless they were as incompetent as Miss Erikson, Holmes and I would be under continual surveillance.

"Very well, Holmes and Watson will stick out in Berlin like sore thumbs. I have operatives everywhere. There are few places they can go and little they can do. We will overnight here in Glen Donich. Loch Naire has nothing to recommend in the way of lodging and dining."

Vera Erikson breathed a sigh of relief.

CHAPTER 13
Things to come

I neither saw the flash nor heard the whoosh. In an instant we were standing in an alley of a bustling city.

"Has it happened?" I asked skeptically.

"Yes, Watson. This is Berlin, 1939. This way. The Blue House is a short walk."

"The Blue House?"

"Our accommodations for the evening."

Fifteen minutes later we were comfortably ensconced in the adjoining rooms of a quaint little hotel called The Blue House, which, to my surprise, wasn't blue at all. As Holmes would later explain, there was a perfectly reasonable explanation for the name.

After I had taken a much-needed bath and joined Holmes for a delicious dinner, we repaired to the balcony outside of his room, I with brandy and he with his pipe. What Holmes had only sketched out earlier, he now filled in with detail.

It was still daylight when Holmes exited the wormhole into the alley behind the Iron John Tavern. He stepped out of the small alcove and gathered his bearings. Across the alley was the back door of the tavern Wells had described. A small sign above the entry read *Eisen John*. He checked his watch as he had done a split second before stepping into what we would both eventually refer to as the time portal. Only a few seconds had passed since entering the portal a thousand miles away and eighteen years earlier.

Holmes walked to the entrance of the alley and looked both ways up and down the street. Next he walked to the corner that was bisected by a much wider and much busier street. He fixed the front entrance of the tavern in his mind. The possibility of discovering what Moriarty was up to seemed a daunting undertaking. He glanced at his watch once again. He couldn't lose track of time. It was imperative he return to Loch Naire before Moriarty arrived. I would not fare well alone with Moriarty and his henchmen. Time was of the essence. Berlin was a large, bustling city. He would need to get his bearings, learn his way around, and hope he could enlist the aid of an ally. But how? Was that feasible with so little time at hand? As he stood looking up and down the street, a bus passed by with Anhalter Bahnhof written on the destination sign. "Of course," Holmes said to himself, "the train station." It was the perfect place with hundreds of people with whom he could blend in. Holmes followed the bus on foot. Half an hour later he found himself standing outside of the impressive station. It was one of Europe's oldest, having first been built in 1839.

Holmes entered the station. Now how to set about finding an ally? He was careful not to draw attention to himself. The person who seemed to be observing instead of being self-absorbed was an easy mark for those trained in picking out individuals who seemed out of place. Recalling Wells' account three years earlier, Holmes could not be sure if an Englishman in 1939 Berlin would be welcomed or not. His instincts told him no. He picked up a discarded newspaper and entered the colossal waiting room. He found a space on a bench that allowed the widest view of travelers waiting for their trains. For twenty minutes Holmes carefully observed everyone coming and going and those seated waiting for their trains. No one fit the bill. Holmes checked his watch again. He should return to the portal, he told himself. Of course what he nor I knew at the time, Moriarty would not arrive in Loch Naire until morning. Holmes made the decision to leave. As he folded his newspaper, a small, but well-dressed older gentleman entered the station and took a seat on the bench opposite Holmes. He sat, made himself comfortable, and opened a book. It was the title of the book that piqued Holmes' interest: *The Secret Sharer* by Joseph Conrad. Nothing unusual about that, after all Conrad was an internationally known writer. What drew Holmes' attention was the fact the title was written in English. Holmes reopened the newspaper and pretended to read, all the while studying the man carefully. His clothing had all the hallmarks of having been tailored on Savile Row. Without question the style was contemporary, but the cut and the fabric were definitely English. There was nothing distinctive about the man's shirt, but his tie was another matter. Unlike the ties being worn by other men in the waiting room, this man's tie was tied with a Windsor knot. While not unusual, the Windsor knot was regarded by many as an affectation. It seemed designed to draw attention to itself and the wearer. As for the suit, it was a common practice for tourists to visit Savile Row and have a tailored suit made. But the most telling feature, in Holmes' opinion, was the shoes. They were custom-made Crockett and Jones brogues of London. Their intricately detailed pattern was unmistakable. They spoke volumes. Holmes was certain he had found his man. One might visit London and buy a suit, but having a pair of shoes custom made was another matter entirely. It suggested to Holmes this was a man who had been in England for a lengthy period of time. His clothing from head to toe was meant to give the impression that he was not a foreigner. Perhaps he was an expat or a traveler on an extended stay. Whatever his reason, the man had been in England long enough to justify a full English wardrobe.

Holmes checked the departure board. Nothing was leaving for at least another three-quarters of an hour. Holmes rose and took a seat next to his mark.

"Conrad, ich sehe," Holmes said. "Sie Conrad gerne?"

"Yes, I do," the man said in excellent English. "The excellence of your German belies only the slightest hint of received pronunciation."

Touché, Holmes thought to himself. "I commend you on your English with the faintest hint of High German."

Both men laughed.

"Allow me to introduce myself, I am Hamish Watson."

"Pleased to meet you Mr. Watson. Darden Poppin."

"Am I correct in surmising you were aware of me before I sat here beside you?"

"Of course, for the same reason you noticed me, the style and cut of your suit. You drew my attention the moment I entered the waiting room. Pretending to read the newspaper without ever turning a page suggested you were here to observe."

Holmes had to be cautious. He was at least half an hour away from the portal. The man he had selected had the bearing of a military man, or perhaps a government agent. He had taken a chance, now he could do nothing but follow through. He must proceed with the utmost caution.

"I have no rational basis for what I am about to ask, but I must take a chance that you are a man I can trust. The next train doesn't leave for another forty minutes. I wonder if there is some place close we could retreat to that would allow us to converse in private?"

Darden Poppin laughed. "If I didn't know better, Mr. Watson, I would think you were American rather than English. If my time in England has taught me anything, it is that an Englishman would never be so bold so soon."

"In my business one has to be bold, Mr. Poppin. Time is of the essence."

"Actually my train doesn't leave for another two hours. There's a beer garden around the corner. We can talk in private there."

Holmes and Darden Poppin exited the station and entered the nearby beer garden. A hostess met them and asked if they would like a table inside or in the garden. "The garden," Poppin said.

The hostess led them outside to the sunny garden. She returned shortly with two steins of beer.

"Now, how can I help you, Mr. Holmes?"

Holmes took a sip of beer and smiled to himself. "Too clever by half, I am afraid."

"With anyone but an Anglophile. Your photo is well known to readers of *The London Times*. But I must confess you look much younger in person than I would have expected. Not to put too fine a point on it, I am quite familiar with the writings of John Hamish Watson. It is both a pleasure and an honor, sir. Now what brings Sherlock Holmes to Berlin in these perilous times, and how may I be of service?"

"I hope I am correct in assuming I can trust you?"

Darden Poppin chuckled. "Should you not be able to, I should hardly admit to that. I think we both know you have little choice. Clearly, you are here on a matter of some urgency."

"I commend you on your deductive skills. You are correct, but I cannot go into detail. Judging by your manner of dress and obvious training abroad, I venture to guess you occupy a position with the government."

"Perhaps the less each of us knows about the other, the better."

"For the time being let us pretend that for the past eighteen years I have suffered from amnesia. I need to know what is going on in the world."

Poppin burst out laughing. "I love the English. I do miss England so. You have such a wry sense of humor."

Holmes wasn't smiling.

"Oh, I see. You're serious!"

"Specifically I need to know what has been going on in Germany since 1936."

"Mr. Holmes, I know you to be fiercely patriotic and a man of unquestioned integrity. Thus I am placing as much trust in you as you are in me. I was born in Germany and I have spent a great deal of time in England working as an *observer*."

The euphemism didn't escape Holmes. He drew down a deep breath. He may have made one of the greatest miscalculations of his life.

"Not to worry, Mr. Holmes. My heart does indeed belong to my homeland, but my loyalty in these troubled times is to England."

"I believe the term is double agent."

"I realize it must sound cloak and dagger, but yes. I am afraid the country I love has fallen under the spell of a madman. His name is Adolph Hitler. He is chancellor of Germany, or, more accurately, dictator of this nation. For the past six years he has gained and consolidated power. His power is organized around a brutal political party referred to as the Nazis."

Poppin confirmed what Wells had shared with Holmes and me during our most recent visit to Sandgate. The Nazis were something new, something we had not seen in our time. "Go on," Holmes said.

"Hitler's aim is simple: destroy all enemies, purify the German race by persecuting and destroying inferior beings, create a superior economy, and build a war machine unlike any seen in history. A secret police force known as The Gestapo or the S.S. enforces Hitler's will in the most barbaric and extreme manner possible."

The very things that would appeal to Moriarty, Holmes thought.

"How has the world responded?"

"Thanks to Neville Chamberlain, the current prime minister, England has engaged in a misguided policy of appeasement. After talks in Munich, Chamberlain naively declared to the world that Hitler was no threat and that the free world should look forward to 'peace for our time.' Since then Germany has annexed Austria, invaded Czechoslovakia, and now has its sights set on Poland. Only a fool believes the remainder of Europe and England are immune from Hitler's reach. That is where we stand, Mr. Holmes. I am deeply troubled. The world has underestimated this threat."

"That is quite a lot to take in."

"You must forgive me, Mr. Holmes. It is incredulous that a man such as you seems to have no awareness of these facts."

"There is a perfectly logical reason, but one that goes far beyond our capacity to understand it."

"I'll take you at your word that there is a reasonable explanation. Will you be in Berlin long?"

"I can't be sure. I have work to do of a personal nature."

"May I be so bold as to enquire if you are here on a case?"

"Yes, a rather challenging one."

"Have you made arrangements for a place to stay?"

"I have only recently arrived."

"What about Dr. Watson? Is he with you?"

"Soon."

"In that case, allow me to suggest a recommendation. There is a small, family owned hotel not far from here called Das Blaue Haus."

"The Blue House," Holmes repeated. "I should seek out a blue hotel."

"No, the hotel is not blue. It is red brick. Blue is a euphemism for sadness. During the great flu outbreak prior to the turn of the century, the hotel served as a morgue. It was once a place of great sadness. But you will find it to your liking. Its former reputation keeps many away, which makes it perfect for those wishing to maintain a low profile while in Berlin. Its proprietors are Ingrid and Max Veidt. When you check in they will view you with suspicion and seem untrustworthy. They will present themselves to you as fervently patriotic Germans. They are not. They can be trusted. But, be careful Mr. Holmes, they can only do so much."

"How will I find you again?" Holmes asked.

"Should it be necessary, Ingrid and Max know how to reach me. It has been a pleasure, Mr. Holmes. I will leave first."

"Two questions before you leave, Mr. Poppin. What do you know of Professor Moriarty?"

"Other than what Dr. Watson has set forth in his chronicles, nothing."

"What about Albert Einstein? You are familiar with him?"

"Mr. Holmes, surely you jest. Who does not know of Einstein?"

"You know where he lives?"

"Of course. He maintains an apartment here in Berlin."

"If I wished to visit him?"

"He works at a top secret military facility. I would not advise attempting to visit him there. He takes dinner every night at a little bistro not far from The Blue House. Ask Max and Ingrid, they will provide you with directions. Now, I really must go. Good luck, Mr. Holmes. Please wait at least fifteen minutes. Auf Wiedersehen."

Darden Poppin exited the beer garden through a back entrance marked for use by employees only.

Holmes finished his beer. Twenty-five minutes later he also exited the beer garden by way of the employee entrance. He followed the bus route back to the alley and re-entered the portal. A moment later he was back in Scotland.

Holmes waved off my offer of a brandy. "That was a bit of rum luck, wasn't it, meeting this Poppin chap?"

"You have no idea, Watson. If Darden Poppin is to be believed, the entire world is teetering on the brink of war."

"If he is to be believed? Do you have reason to doubt him?"

"No, only there is much more we must find out."

"How Moriarty figures into this, you mean?"

"Yes. I have been wrestling with that question. It may be—I emphasize *may*—that the future Moriarty has no connection to this at all."

"The future Moriarty?" I put down my drink. "I am not following."

"Hold onto your hat, old chap. We are about to enter a realm far beyond our abilities to comprehend. I believe there are two Moriartys."

"Two? Good lord. What on earth do you mean, Holmes?"

"As there are two of you and two of me."

"I may have to have another bottle of brandy sent up."

"Consider, Watson, you and I can reasonably expect to be alive eighteen years from now."

"Barring an accident or an unforeseen illness, yes, that is a reasonable expectation."

"We have traveled forward in time to 1939, yet we have not aged. We are now as we were. Although we are in Berlin, we could as easily be in London."

"I suppose."

"Would it not stand to reason that if you and I were to travel to London and visit 221 B, Baker Street, we should meet ourselves?"

"Don't be ridiculous, Holmes. You are being completely—that is-" I suddenly felt as if I had tumbled into the proverbial rabbit hole. "Holmes, are you suggesting we exist in a parallel time?"

"Not parallel, but we must acknowledge that the future is its own reality. If we accept that, then we must accept that you and I and Moriarty also exist in that reality."

I finished off the remainder of my brandy and poured myself another. "Holmes, this is science fantasy."

"I grant you it is difficult to accept. Whether we understand what has happened or not, you and I are here in Berlin in 1939. We have traveled from our own time eighteen years into the future. If John Watson and Sherlock Holmes are indeed alive in 1939, they occupy an existence and reality quite apart from our own. If they don't exist, Watson, then they are dead. The same will be true of Moriarty."

"Earlier you said the older Moriarty might not be involved. Are you suggesting he may have given up his life of crime?"

"Possible, however unlikely. His existence in 1939 may be far removed from that of the younger Moriarty."

"Then we can't even be sure the older Moriarty is here in Germany."

"Correct."

"Holmes, if indeed our future selves are alive and well in London in 1939, do they have memories of what we are doing now?"

Holmes did not immediately answer, but took his time considering my question. Finally he said, "What a brilliant question, Watson."

"Really?"

"In other words, were we able to interview ourselves, would we discover the answers to all of our questions?"

"Yes, something like that."

"I couldn't possibly venture a guess."

I poured the last drop of brandy from the decanter as Holmes tapped out the cold ash from his clay pipe. Berlin spread before us like a glittering sea at night, its thousands of lights reflecting in the low hanging clouds above the city. Holmes' story and his speculations were both fascinating and unsettling. "It is almost as it were fated," I said, returning to that spectacular bit of good fortune meeting Darden Poppin.

"Indeed," Holmes said without much enthusiasm.

For Holmes, luck was something to distrust, something to be suspicious of. He had yet to say, but I sensed he believed that meeting Darden Poppin was too serendipitous. Holmes had gone to the station to find someone who spoke English, but to have met Poppin, who had proved so informative and so helpful was too convenient. Such good fortune was the type of thing he struggled with. My war experiences left me with an entirely different view. I was more than familiar with serendipity. There are times when one must simply accept luck, or good fortune, or whatever one wished to call it, and move on. There was simply no accounting for the sibylline. I finished off the last little drop of brandy in my glass.

I knew that Holmes was churning over the mass of information he had collected, trying to sort the variables. I lacked those deductive skills that were his lifeblood, but I knew human nature. Holmes was unsettled. He was staring at that puzzle he had alluded to. There were too many pieces. He had yet to see the picture he was trying to piece together. He rose and leaned against the balcony, looking down on the city before us. "Let us turn in old chap, we have a busy day ahead."

CHAPTER 14
Past meets future

My lack of sleep from the previous nights proved the tonic. I slept like a baby. After a hearty breakfast, Holmes and I spent most of the day in the vicinity of the inn. We took to the streets of Berlin but kept to ourselves. One could not help but be struck by the differences in the styles of clothing, automobiles, and architecture. Holmes cautioned me not to become too fixated on these things as my curiosity might draw unwanted attention to us. "As it is," he said, "our clothes already set us apart from the locals."

Berlin, I supposed, looked as any large European city did in 1939. Life seemed to progress as normal. Among the general population, one did not sense impending war. The occasional appearances of soldiers and military vehicles, however, told another tale.

Our goal for the evening was simple: attempt to meet with Professor Einstein. In retrospect, I had to admit to myself I had rather enjoyed our first meeting with the Professor. He had given me much to think about. At the time it was all too much to take in, but now that Holmes and I had been miraculously transported to the future, my estimation of the Professor rose considerably.

As is typical of many men of science, Einstein was a creature of habit and routine. At six o'clock that evening, we would insinuate ourselves on Einstein at Maganhildi's Bakery and Restaurant.

At the appointed time Holmes and I made the short journey from The Blue House to the little restaurant where Einstein took his dinner.

"Here we are, Watson, 27 Wilmetstraße." The sign above the tavern door read Maganhildi's Bäckerei und

Restaurant. Holmes peered through the establishment window. "Poppin was right. There he is." He pointed to the table furthest from the window.

"Poppin?"

"Einstein, Watson!"

I peered through the window and positively gasped. "Holmes, are you sure that's him?"

"Without a doubt."

"Good lord, what's happened to the man? Look at his hair. He's an old man."

"Watson, this is not the Einstein you and I met in London a few days ago. This is Albert Einstein eighteen years later."

"Well, if his appearance is any indication of what has happened to the two of us, let us steer well clear of Baker Street."

Holmes chuckled. "Come, let us have a visit with our old friend."

Holmes and I entered the restaurant. A bell above the door tinkled. Einstein was the only patron. Immediately a pleasant looking woman whom I presumed to be Maganhildi greeted us. "Guten Abend. Willkommen, meine Herren."

"Danke," Holmes said in what sounded to me flawless German.

"Bitte nehmen Sie Platz."

"Herr Einstein erwartet uns."

"Sehr gut." The hostess nodded and led us to Einstein's table.

The transformation between the Einstein we had met only days ago and the one we were looking at now was startling. Instead of the vibrant young man we had met previously with short, well coiffed hair, this Einstein was considerably older in appearance, heavier, and had alarmingly wild hair, as if he had just been electrocuted.

"May we join you, Professor?"

Einstein looked up from the bowl of soup he was dining on and dabbed his white, bushy moustache with a napkin. "Do I know you gentlemen?"

"You don't remember us?" I asked reflexively, suddenly realizing how easy it was to fall into that time trap. Of course he didn't recall. The last time he saw us was eighteen years earlier.

"My apologies, I am afraid I do not recall."

"Sherlock Holmes and Dr. Watson. London. 1921."

The hostess returned to the table with leather bound menus.

"Oh, thank—er—Danke!" I corrected myself.

Einstein closed his eyes and pressed his fingers against his temples, as if to divine the past. His eyes opened. "Sherlock Holmes and Dr. Watson? But—but, of course, but that was years ago. You have hardly changed at all. How is that possible?"

"Yes, we will get to that shortly," Holmes said brusquely.

Einstein gestured for us to sit. "But what are you doing here? Berlin is not a hospitable place for foreigners these days."

"So we have been told. I'll come to the point. You remember your abduction in England in 1921?"

"Of course, as if it were yesterday."

"For some of us it practically was yesterday, Professor." I had a little chuckle at Einstein's expense.

"Doctor, if you please."

"Yes?"

"I am speaking of myself. I am no longer a professor. I am a doctor."

"Pardon me."

Holmes was growing impatient. "Doctor—"

"Yes?" Einstein and I responded in unison.

"I believe your abduction in 1921 may have some bearing on what you are working on now."

"My abduction?"

The hostess returned to our table. "Sind Sie bereit zu Bestellen?"

"Zwei Kaffee mit Milch," Holmes said. The hostess nodded and collected the two menus. A moment later she disappeared into the kitchen.

"Your German is very good, Mr. Holmes."

"Thank you, Doctor."

"What did you order?" I asked.

"Two coffees with milk."

"I think I would have preferred tea."

"We are attempting to avoid attracting attention, Watson."

"Right!"

"Mr. Holmes, I have a lot of questions, first among them, why are you here?"

"To even the casual observer one can see Germany is preparing for war. It is reasonable to assume you are part of that effort."

Einstein pushed his soup bowl away. "My work is classified."

"Classified?" I said.

"Top secret, Watson."

"I know what classified means. You will recall I served in the Army."

Holmes pressed on. "It is most important, Doctor. I am not asking you to divulge secrets. If you will just give me some sense of what your work entails."

"Mr. Holmes, I simply cannot discuss my work with you. It is a matter of national importance. I must ask you to refrain from further questions. If you persist, I will have to report you to my superiors. It is only out of respect for you and our former acquaintance that stops me from doing so." Einstein rose, laid a few banknotes on the table and bid us adieu.

The bell above the entrance door tinkled.

"Shouldn't you pursue him?"

"Yes, but we must find another way to approach him. We must know what Einstein is working on, Watson. I believe this is the key to everything."

"Here's our cof—" I stopped short. The woman standing behind us was not our hostess. Nor was she holding a tray.

"Good evening, gentlemen."

"I would say it is a pleasure to see you again, Miss Erikson, but it is not."

"However, I am most glad to see you again, Mr. Holmes."

"How did you find us?" I snapped. "Have you been following us?"

"Following you, Doctor?" Professor Moriarty entered with a pistol and stood beside Miss Erikson.

"That explains the smell coming from the kitchen," Holmes said.

"You have not be followed, Dr. Watson. You have been led."

Holmes' intuition about Darden Poppin proved correct.

"Unfortunately, your past has caught up with you, Mr. Holmes. You should have stayed clear of the portal. Your next trip through the portal will be your last, I am afraid."

"I believe you spoke similar words at Reichenbach Falls."

"Outside!"

"Why not shoot them now?" Vera Erikson asked, waving a lethal looking pistol.

"Not here, nor now."

"Why not?"

"Do not argue with me, Miss Erikson. We shall take them back to the portal and dispatch them as soon as we arrive in Scotland."

"Suit yourself."

"At least give us the courtesy of knowing your plan," Holmes said.

"I think not."

"How are we supposed to know what you're up to if you don't tell us?" I asked out of curiosity and stalling for time.

"I said no!"

"Why not? You have the upper hand," Holmes said mockingly.

"You are trying to provoke me Mr. Holmes in the faulty belief that you will distract me and buy yourself some time."

"Since you're going to kill them anyway, what difference does it make?" Vera Erikson asked.

"Stay out of this!"

"You must have a reason not to tell."

"Not knowing something keeps this man awake at night. I can think of no better way to send him to his death than by not knowing why."

Vera Erikson crossed her arms. "It seems a bit silly to me."

"What you think is not important. I shall put them in handcuffs while you bring the car around back. Lock the door behind you as you leave."

"Very well." Vera Erikson went to the door, turned the open sign to closed and set the lock. The bell above her head tinkled as she exited into the dark, cold night.

"She is right, you know." Holmes was looking for a crack in Moriarty's concentration to make a move.

"I know your game, Mr. Holmes."

"And I know yours, Professor. Even you have some sense of fair play. Humor a condemned man."

"Not that it can make any difference now. The past has already been changed, Mr. Holmes."

"Changed? How?" I asked.

"As a result of Einstein's trip to America, he eventually emigrated to the United States, settled in New Jersey, and deprived helping Germany develop the atomic bomb."

"The atomic bomb?" What on Earth was Moriarty talking about?

"Yes, Doctor. The atomic bomb is a weapon unlike any the world has ever seen. Whichever country develops the bomb first will dominate the world."

"But Einstein never made the trip to America," I said.

"Precisely, Watson. The professor made sure of that."

"Correct, Mr. Holmes. Instead of working for the Americans, Einstein is here in the fatherland where he belongs."

"You traveled into the future and back to make a man miss a boat trip?"

"One has to be careful, Doctor. Time is fragile. It is not wise to effect big changes. Otherwise there might be unanticipated consequences."

At that moment the most miraculous thing happened. Jane Wells burst in from the kitchen holding a pistol. "Drop your weapon, Professor Martyarty!"

"Jane!" I cried.

The instant Moriarty turned toward Jane, Holmes lunged and twisted the pistol out of Moriarty's hand.

"It is Moriarty you moron!"

"I believe this is one of those unanticipated consequences, Professor. Excellent timing, Mrs. Wells!"

"Thank you, Mr. Holmes, I just had to make sure you and Doctor Watson were safe. Bertie is waiting for us outside."

"How could you have possibly found us here?" I asked.

"After you and Mr. Holmes left Sandgate, Bertie and I had a sit down. I told him if anything happened to you and Mr. Holmes, he would be responsible. He agreed. So here we are."

"Yes," I said warily. "But how did you find us here?"

"When we arrived at the portal, we ran into a vagabond who said something strange had just happened. A man and woman went into the clearing and never came out. We went in right after them. When we arrived, there they were turning the corner, so we followed them here."

Moriarty shook his head. "I gave that man a five pound note to keep his mouth shut."

Jane Wells smiled delightfully. "All it cost me was a peck on the cheek."

"We haven't any more time to waste. We are grateful to you Mrs. Wells. Watson, I will take care of the Professor. You return to England with Herbert and Jane. Get in touch with Professor Einstein and tell him everything you know."

"What about you?"

"I will pay another visit to the Einstein on this end. This time I shall attempt to be more persuasive. Move along, Professor."

Holmes led Moriarty at gunpoint into the kitchen.

Jane Wells and I hurried outside. "This way," she pointed. "If we go that way we will run into that wicked woman who's with that horrible man."

We took another corner and there was H.G. Wells astride a motorcycle with a sidecar attached. Wells was dressed in a soldier's uniform. "Hello," he said. "Hop in. This was the best I could do on the spur of the moment."

I climbed into the tiny seat of the sidecar. It was obviously designed for one passenger.

"You don't mind if I sit on your lap, do you?"

Before I could answer, Jane wells bunched her dress together and hopped onto my lap. "Well, I-- No, not at all." My heart was racing. "Wells, where did you come up with this?"

"We took it from some Nazi chaps. I must tell you, they were very angry."

Wells kick started the bike and immediately it roared to life. "Grab your hat," he yelled. "We're off." The front wheel hopped off the ground and we were on our way. Immediately, my hat flew off. From behind us came the rapid-fire sound of a machine gun. Bullets shot past us with eerie closeness. "Hold on, they're chasing us." Wells ripped open a side holster and pulled a pistol from it. "Here, take this, Doctor!"

I took the pistol from Wells and began firing blindly behind me into the dark.

Jane Wells threw her arms around my neck. "Oh, this is dreadfully exciting! Don't you think so, Doctor?"

"No," I cried, "those are real bullets they are shooting at us!" The rear light of the motorcycle exploded in a shower of shattered glass and the clink, clink of bullets peppered the sidecar. I felt quite lucky to be alive.

Within a matter of minutes we arrived at the alley concealing the portal. Jane and I hopped out of the sidecar while Wells tore off the uniform he had absconded. Ripping off the leather strap that secured his motorbike goggles, Wells wrapped the strap around the throttle of the idling motorcycle and kicked it into gear. At once the motorbike roared off without a driver, flying pell-mell down the street. A moment later there was a horrible crash and explosion as it plowed into a parked military vehicle. "That will keep those bloody Nazis busy," Wells said catching up with us in the alley. Each of us entered the portal one after the other.

A moment later we were standing in front of the two giant stones in Scotland.

Vera Erikson waited impatiently behind the wheel of the running Mercedes sedan. The heater was barely generating any warmth against the biting cold. What was that earth-shaking explosion and what was taking Moriarty so long? This was so typical of him. He might be a criminal genius, but the man spent entirely too much time talking. For all she knew, he might be sitting down with Sherlock Holmes over a cup a coffee. She blew hot breath onto her hands and furiously rubbed them together. That was it. She had finally had enough.

She stormed back to the front of the restaurant before remembering she had locked the door. She peered through the glass. The dining room was empty. The Professor must be in the kitchen, she decided. Traipsing around the building to the alley, she entered through the back door. The rope she had used to tie up Maganhildi and the cook was now wrapped around Moriarty.

He was sitting on the floor with his back against the stove. A gag made from his own scarf was tied securely over his mouth.

"Professor? Professor? What happened?"

Moriarty tried to speak through the gag. Vera Erikson couldn't understand a word.

"What was that?"

Moriarty tried again unsuccessfully to speak.

"Oh!" Miss Erikson pulled the gag loose.

"Untie me, you idiot. What have you been doing?"

Miss Erikson busied herself with the rope. "You said to wait in the car, but it was getting cold."

"I know what I said."

"What happened?"

Moriarty threw off the rope and scrambled to his feet. "What do you think happened?"

"I can't imagine."

"It was that stupid Wells woman."

"What's she doing here?"

"How should I know? She should have stayed home and minded her own business. Is the car ready?"

"Yes, where are we going?"

"You are going back to London. Dr. Watson will be on his way to Einstein's apartment."

"What should I do when I see him?"

"Shoot him!"

"Einstein or the Doctor?"

"Watson, you dolt!"

Vera Erikson was becoming quite tired of Moriarty's insults. He might be a criminal genius, but he had no idea how to treat a woman.

"I will follow Sherlock Holmes. When you arrive in Loch Naire, make sure to arrange transportation for me."

Vera Erikson and Moriarty went in separate directions, she to the portal and he to Einstein's Berlin apartment.

Vera Erikson shook her head. Not once had she heard the man say thank you.

CHAPTER 15
One foot in the future

Einstein's apartment was a short walk from Maganhildi's Restaurant. As Darden Poppin had said, Max and Ingrid Veidt had proved invaluable. Holmes easily found the address he had committed to memory. He didn't have much time. Soon Vera Erikson would find Moriarty tied up in the kitchen and release him. At the most he had ten minutes.

Holmes climbed the three flights of stairs to Einstein's apartment and knocked with some urgency on the door.

The door swung open. Einstein was dressed in the old sweater that would appear in so many photographs in later years. He sighed. "Mr. Holmes, you are becoming most tiresome. I thought I made it clear to you we have nothing more to say. As you seem not to respect my wishes, you leave me no choice but to call the authorities."

Einstein left Holmes standing in the doorway and went to the telephone on the sideboard. He picked up the receiver and began to dial. Holmes approached the sideboard, followed the trail of the telephone wire and ripped it from the wall. The telephone went dead.

"I am sorry, Doctor, but I have little time. Professor Moriarty will be here any moment."

Einstein hung up the receiver of the now useless telephone. "Moriarty? Who is Moriarty?"

"He is a criminal mastermind who has changed your life in ways you cannot comprehend."

"Mr. Holmes, forgive me, but I am beginning to question your grip on reality."

"I need you to listen to me carefully, Doctor. I will be brief. You recall our discussions after your kidnapping about wormholes?"

"Vaguely, but that was years ago."

"Time will not allow me to go into specifics. Trust me when I tell you the wormhole is not a theory. An actual wormhole exists in Scotland and comes out here in Berlin. Professor Moriarty has used it, as have I and Dr. Watson, which accounts for the reason Dr. Watson and I appear to you as we did in 1921."

Einstein opened the door to the sideboard and removed a bottle of Schnapps. He filled the glass to the brim. "Would you care for a drink, Mr. Holmes?"

"I haven't time."

"You haven't time? Is that English humor, Mr. Holmes?"

"No, Doctor, this is not a laughing matter. Until I experienced travel through the portal itself, the wormhole was nothing but a theory. Intriguing, to be sure, but little more than a scientific fiction. I assure you the portal exists."

"Were I to believe you, how can you be sure you can return?"

"H.G. Wells used it three years ago. Moriarty has used it several times. And I have used it twice. Each time one arrives within seconds of departing eighteen years later or eighteen years earlier."

"And you wish me to return to London with you?"

"No, Doctor, if memory serves, you said yourself that is quite impossible. Time flows in only one direction."

"Right," Einstein said. "The ball on the tether."

"Which is why someone from the present cannot accidentally stumble into the portal. For them the entrance to the portal does not exist."

"So this Professor Moriarty who is on his way here now intends to do me harm?"

"No, he is coming for me, Doctor."

"He has no interest in me?"

"He is very much interested in you. He will do whatever it takes to keep you safe. He has one goal and one goal only. That is to ensure that you and the other scientists you collaborate with continue working on the development of the weapon you call the atomic bomb."

"Mr. Holmes, you are in possession of information that is highly classified. For your own safety, I advise you to leave immediately. All I will say is Germany is under constant threat from our enemies. This matter is concluded."

"I realize the futility of attempting to convince you otherwise. Moriarty's knowledge of the past has allowed him to change a significant event in your life."

"How did he accomplish that?"

Holmes glanced at his watch. "America and Germany embarked on a program to develop the atomic bomb at approximately the same time."

"That is common knowledge, Mr. Holmes. Our spies tell us the program in America is referred to as The Manhattan Project. The Americans are far behind us in the development of atomic weapons."

"Because of you, Doctor. After Moriarty arrived here in Berlin, he discovered that your journey to America was the catalyst for you to remain in America and to eventually begin the work that would lead to the successful development of the atomic bomb."

"And that didn't happen, did it, Mr. Holmes? Because I never took that trip to America."

"Exactly! And now you know the reason why you were inexplicably kidnapped and no harm came to you."

"If I am understanding you correctly, this Professor Moriarty ensures that Germany will make one of the greatest scientific breakthroughs in history by making me miss an ocean voyage to America?"

"I am quite aware of how ridiculous this sounds. Instead of working in America, you are here in Germany helping a madman develop a weapon that will change the course of history."

"And you would like to me to abandon my work and flee Germany?"

"Yes."

"Mr. Holmes, I have the greatest respect for you. These are perilous times, and I know that our enemies will go to any lengths to undermine our government. The British are well-known for their preposterous attempts to plant misinformation or to turn the course of events. It saddens me to see that you have become a pawn in their attempts to weaken our nation. We have nothing more to discuss, Mr. Holmes."

A sudden breeze blew through the opened apartment door.

"That will no doubt be Professor Moriarty having just entered downstairs," Holmes said.

For a moment neither Holmes nor Einstein knew what would happen next. Despite their differences, both men felt a great deal of admiration for the other and immeasurable respect.

"There is a back way, Mr. Holmes. A door from my kitchen leads to a small balcony and fire escape. Good luck."

"Thank you." Holmes paused in the doorway to the kitchen "One last thing, Doctor! Are you quite confident your allegiances are in the best interests of the world?"

"I am a German, Mr. Holmes. You are an Englishman. We both come from very proud nations. I daresay we would both defend our homelands to the death."

Holmes slipped quietly out of Einstein's apartment and made his way back to the portal.

CHAPTER 16
One foot in the past

I said my goodbyes to Jane and H.G. Wells at King's Cross Station. "Perhaps we shall meet again."

Wells shook my hand. "I hope so, Doctor."

I offered my hand to Jane, which she promptly ignored and gave me a small kiss on the cheek. "I will miss you, Dr. Watson."

I felt myself blush. I couldn't help but think Jane Wells was a woman perhaps better suited for the future. She seemed not to be constrained by the stiff conventions of London in 1921.

With so much excitement and the long train journey back to London from Loch Naire, the three of us were exhausted. I was thankful I had only a short taxi ride to Belgravia. Jane and Herbert still had a few more hours of travel ahead of them. We waved goodbye and I hired a taxi outside of the station. The ride home allowed me to clear my thoughts and to plan for my meeting with the young Professor Einstein.

Upon entering my apartment, I discovered a note from Mrs. Portland.

Dr. Watson:

As your schedule has been anything but predictable these past several days, I have been in a quandary regarding meals. I have prepared a couple of cold dishes for you in the event you return home when I am not here. Everything else is in order and laid out for you.

Mrs. P.

Thinking on that innocent peck on the cheek by Jane Wells and the concern exhibited by Mrs. Portland, I felt myself becoming a bit misty eyed and melancholy regarding the emptiness I felt since the passing of Mrs. Watson. Holmes was a confirmed bachelor for whom the companionship of a woman was of no necessity. Other than his brief flirtation with Irene Adler years earlier, Holmes found enough in life to keep him occupied. I, on the other hand, felt incomplete without the companionship of a woman. Whether romance would find its way to me again or not, I could not guess, but I would remain open to the possibility.

After enjoying the meal Mrs. Portland had put aside for me, I nursed a glass of Port in front of a crackling fire. Afterward I turned in for a welcome and excellent night's rest. Before drifting off, it occurred to me I might wake in the morning having discovered that I had had the most vivid and unusual dream.

I awoke to the sound of Mrs. Portland preparing breakfast. "I am glad to see you, Dr. Watson," Mrs. Portland said as I seated myself at the table.

"Thank you, Mrs. Portland, I am glad to see you as well."

Mrs. Portland, who didn't smile often, smiled. "Thank you." She placed the morning paper on the table to my right and went about her business.

After finishing my morning rituals and dressing, I set off across London by taxi. Wells had given me Einstein's London address on the journey from Scotland, as they had communicated frequently during their preparations for their aborted trip to America.

I ascended the steps to Einstein's apartment and knocked on the door. Einstein himself answered, appearing a little more than surprised. "Dr. Watson! How unexpected."

"Forgive me," I said, removing my hat. "I wonder if I might have a word." I stepped forward into the doorway to forestall any excuse Einstein might have for turning me away. "It is a matter of extreme urgency."

"Please." Einstein gestured for me to come inside. He took my hat and overcoat. "May I offer you something?" He asked, indicating for me to sit.

"No, thank you."

Einstein sat across from me. "Now, what is this matter of great urgency?"

"It concerns the wormhole."

Einstein shook his head and laughed. "Doctor, I find it difficult to understand why you and Mr. Holmes are obsessed with this idea. As I conveyed to you both previously, wormholes are a scientific theory. There is a very good chance they exist, but they are beyond our current capabilities to prove their existence. One day perhaps we will have the means, but for now they remain theoretical."

"No, Professor, you are quite wrong."

Einstein looked at me as if I had just slapped him across the face and he needed a second or two to process what had happened. "Dr. Watson, I intend no disrespect. You are clearly a man of advanced intelligence and skill, but, and I say this in the most humble way possible, you are speaking to Albert Einstein."

"Professor, I also intend no disrespect. Unlike you, a theorist, I have experienced travel through a wormhole. I assure you, one exists."

Einstein burst out laughing. "You British do make me laugh." Einstein rose to show me out. "It is nice to see you again, Doctor, but I really must get about my work. Please give my regards to Mr. Holmes."

I remained seated. "I cannot pass along your greeting to Holmes as he is currently in Berlin."

"Berlin?" Einstein asked, now seemingly interested. "What is he doing in Berlin?"

"Actually, he is meeting with you eighteen years into the future. You are working on a top secret project."

Einstein went to the buffet and poured two glasses of whisky. He returned to his chair and offered me one of the glasses. It was still quite early in the day for whisky.

"Very well, Doctor, you have my attention."

"The entrance to the portal is on the outskirts of the small Scottish town of Loch Naire. How he managed it, I don't know, but Wells worked out the location. He made the discovery three years ago."

"Wells never told me."

"He never told anyone. He felt it was too dangerous. It was his wife Jane who contacted Sherlock Holmes. Holmes was the one who saw the relationship between a series of disparate events that encouraged Wells to share his experience."

"You do realize how fantastical your story sounds! Are you sure you aren't being taken in? Wells is quite the storyteller."

"Were it not for the fact that I have traveled through the wormhole myself, I would not believe a single word of what I am telling you."

"For the moment I will give you the benefit of the doubt."

"Very kind of you," I replied.

"Such a thing would be one of the greatest—if not the greatest--scientific discoveries in history. What is the urgency you speak of?"

"Germany in 1939 is preparing for another world war. A brutal dictator has become chancellor. I don't believe it is an understatement to say his plan is to conquer the world."

"That is somewhat hyperbolic, wouldn't you say?"

"In another context, perhaps. Over the years Holmes and I have crossed paths with one of the most sinister criminal minds on the planet. His name is Professor Moriarty. Holmes refers to him as The Napoleon of Crime."

"Doctor, I really do not have time for this. I have a lot to do."

"All right, Professor, then I will get right to the point. You become a willing participant in what may well result in the destruction of the free world as we know it."

"Even if I did believe this preposterous story, I would never agree to become party to such a thing."

"In the future, Professor, you don't have a choice. Moriarty has manipulated events. You and other scientists are working on a top secret weapon called the atomic bomb."

The glass Einstein was holding slipped through his fingers and shattered on the floor. "My God," he gasped. "It can be done!"

"Germany and America are neck in neck in the development of this weapon, and you are the catalyst. You were kidnapped for no other reason than to miss that voyage to America."

Einstein appeared stunned. "We have already explored that notion, Doctor. I refuse to believe that was the reason I was kidnapped."

"Do you have a more plausible explanation?"

"I assume it was an extortion scheme that went awry. I have been greatly entertained, Doctor. Once you write this adventure, then some evening when I have little to do, I will purchase a copy of *The Strand* and abandon myself to your fertile imagination."

"How may I convince you?"

"You cannot. Now, I have suitcases to pack."

"You are going on a trip?"

"That is usually why people pack suitcases."

"You are going to America?"

"No, Doctor, that ship has sailed. I will be traveling to Berlin and then home."

"You can't do that. You are playing into Moriarty's plan."

"I can and I will."

"I forbid it."

"How will you stop me?"

I slipped my hand deep into my coat pocket. "I have a gun in my pocket."

"Oh, don't be ridiculous. It's probably just your finger."

There was a knock at the door.

"Hello," I said. "Who's that?"

"You English are so funny. Why don't you open the door and see? It is your friend Sherlock Holmes, no doubt."

I threw open the door and there stood Vera Erikson.

"Hello, boys," she said barging right into Einstein's living room uninvited

"Great Scott! What are you doing here?"

"Who is this woman," Einstein demanded.

"Vera Erikson. She works for Professor Moriarty, and she is quite dangerous."

"Nice to see you again, Doctor. Thank you for the compliment."

"You can't just barge into my apartment uninvited. What are you doing here?" Einstein demanded.

"Professor Moriarty sent me here to bring you back to Germany."

"I don't need an escort. I have already booked passage on a steamer. I was just about to pack my bags."

"You can forget about packing. We are not traveling by steamer."

"I am not traveling anywhere with you. I am a married man."

"What about Holmes?" I broke in.

"I expect the Professor has taken care of Mr. Holmes, just as I am about to take care of you, Doctor." Vera Erikson pulled a pistol out of her wrap.

Einstein's mouth fell open. "You're an assassin?"

"Those were Moriarty's orders. Shoot the Doctor, bring you back to Germany."

"I don't even know this Moriarty. For a man I haven't met, he seems to be very involved in my business. What does he want with me?"

"Insurance. To make sure the future Dr. Einstein doesn't suddenly get cold feet."

"The future Dr. Einstein? I'm a doctor?" Einstein dropped into his chair and ran his hands through his short hair. His mind raced in an attempt to organize everything he heard into something coherent.

"We don't have all day," Vera Erikson said impatiently.

"No, that is impossible."

"Not impossible. Pack a small bag and we'll be on our way. You can purchase clothes when you get to Berlin, otherwise you'll look terribly old fashioned."

"I am speaking of The Pauli Exclusion Principle. Have you heard of that?"

Vera Erikson shook her head. "Is that supposed to mean something to me?"

It meant nothing to me.

"The Exclusion Principle is a theory that says two objects cannot occupy the same space at the same time."

"Very nice. When you get to Berlin, you and your science mates can have a good jaw about it."

"You have no idea what I am talking about, do you?"

Vera Erikson shook her head. "No, I have no idea, nor do I care. I leave those sorts of things to the Einstein's of the world."

"Simply put, it means that if I meet myself in the future, we will both cease to exist."

"Does that mean you explode? You disappear? What?"

"I don't know about that. It's a theory."

"Then I shouldn't worry about it, if I were you."

"Regardless, I am not going with you."

"Then I will have to shoot you!"

Einstein burst out laughing. "You will shoot me? How silly is that, you foolish woman. If you do that, then there won't be an Einstein in 1939."

"I hadn't thought of that. Regardless, you still have to come with me."

I slipped my hand deep into my coat pocket. "Put that gun down, or I'll shoot."

"Don't make me laugh, Dr. Watson. That's not a gun. That's your finger."

"Stand back! I mean it!"

"Don't be ridiculous. That's a Savile Row coat you're wearing."

Vera raised the pistol and took aim. Before she could squeeze off a shot, my coat pocket erupted into an explosion of threads and smoke. The shot got her in the stomach.

Vera Erikson looked down at the spreading bloodstain across her abdomen and then looked up at me. "That was a nice coat, Doctor." Vera Erikson dropped to her knees, drew a final breath and collapsed on the floor.

I took off my coat a laid it over her. I had seen enough death for a lifetime.

Einstein was in a state of shock.

"Professor, I had hoped to convince you. If this doesn't, nothing will. I must return to Berlin. Holmes is in danger."

"I am coming with you, Doctor"

"I don't think that's such a good idea, the least of which is the theory you just described."

"Until proven otherwise, it is just a theory."

"I don't think so. I think you should stay here and reconsider traveling to America."

"Doctor you have spent a great deal of time trying to convince me the wormhole is real. I believe you. As a scientist, I must see it for myself. I am traveling with you whether you agree or not."

"I cannot guarantee your safety. I'm a marked man, Professor."

While Einstein packed a bag, I telephoned Scotland Yard. Inspector Lestrade had a dozen questions I didn't have time to answer. I told him where he would find the body of Vera Erikson and that I would explain all as soon as possible.

Returning to the portal by train was out of the question. It would take hours to reach Loch Naire. We would try our luck at the Croydon Aerodrome.

Einstein and I traveled by train to Croydon and then by taxi to the aerodrome. Once two separate airfields, the Beddington and Waddon aerodromes were now combined into a single entity each located on opposite sides of Plough Lane, a well-traveled thoroughfare. Beddington Aerodrome had been built in 1915 to defend against the German zeppelin raids that had decimated much of London during the war. With the rapid expansion of the aviation industry, Waddon Aerodrome opened in 1918. Shortly after the war ended, the two aerodromes merged and became Croydon Aerodrome, which served as London's main airport and the hub of international air traffic for several years. Lately the aviation business had fallen on hard times. A combination of factors had contributed to its failure: a shaky post war economy, a decline in air travel, exorbitant operating costs, and the bankruptcies of several manufacturers and air services. Until such time as the industry could rebound, there were plenty of unemployed pilots and flying enthusiasts ready at a moment's notice to take to the skies.

It didn't take us long to find half a dozen chaps willing to fly us to Scotland, but none who had a plane capable of transporting a pilot and two passengers. One chap was certain Einstein and I could fit into his passenger cockpit designed for one. He had done it several times, he insisted. Einstein was of lesser build than I, but it didn't take a man of science to know that he and I could not squeeze into that tiny space. "Thank you anyway," I said. "We have no choice but to take the train."

"Wait!" The disappointed fellow said. "If it's worth a bob to you, I know a chap who has what you're looking for."

It seems I had become a veritable bank teller distributing money to all extortionists at will. After parting with yet another pound note, the pilot directed us to a pub located inside a disused hangar. To say the least, the pub was inelegant. Old aircraft parts lay about in addition to a pair of planes no longer in service. Despite its odd appearance, the pub was filled with patrons.

We approached the counter and ordered two pints. "We are looking for Maddox Dayton," I said, pushing two shillings across the counter.

"Who?" The proprietor asked. "Maddox?"

"Dayton," I repeated. "He has a three-seater plane."

"Oh, Mayday. Yeah, I know him. He's the one with the Sopwith Three-seater. You can find him in the corner. Be right back with your change."

"Why do you think he's called Mayday?" Einstein asked.

I preferred not to consider the obvious. "No doubt as a child he couldn't articulate all the syllables in his name."

"Yes," Einstein nodded. "That makes sense."

"Ta, gents." The proprietor slapped down my change.

Einstein and I took our drinks and moved to the corner window with a view of the landing field.

"Excuse me, are you Maddox Dayton?" I asked of the man sporting three day's worth of beard and hair that had yet to be introduced to a brush.

"Mayday, that's what my friends call me."

"John Watson," I said, offering my hand. "This is my friend Albert. May we join you?"

"As you can see, I'm rather busy nursing this pint."

"This is a matter of extreme importance. We understand you have a plane capable of flying three. We will pay you generously for a flight to Scotland."

Maddox Dayton wiped his mouth with the back of his hand and pushed the nearly full pint away. "Some other time, darling."

While Maddox Dayton fueled his plane, my thoughts turned once again to Moriarty. He had expended a great deal of effort to get Einstein to the portal. Were it not for the fact that I had dispatched Miss Erikson, he would have succeeded. By allowing Einstein to travel with me, was I not playing into Moriarty's hands? I was practically delivering him on a platter. If we were under surveillance, it was imperative that we disabuse our watchers of the belief that Einstein and I would do anything other than part company at the aerodrome. I pulled Einstein aside and shared my hastily formed plan. We made a big show of saying goodbye. Einstein shook my hand and got into a taxi that immediately drove away. I remained inside the pub finishing off my pint. Approximately fifteen minutes later, Maddox Dayton taxied to a stop outside of the pub. He gave me a thumbs up and I headed for the waiting plane.

"Climb aboard, Doctor."

I hopped onto the wing and climbed into the front cockpit. A few minutes later Maddox Dayton streaked down the runway and we were airborne and on our way to Scotland.

From high above I looked down on the aerodrome and the network of roads that connected it to London. In the distance the taxi carrying Einstein crept slowly along the winding roads.

The canvas engine cover lying on the empty seat next me rustled. I pulled it aside and there was Einstein. He sat up in his seat a beamed triumphantly. "Well done, Doctor. If I were being followed, my pursuers will follow that empty taxi all the way to my flat in Chelsea."

Our plan had been quite simple. The taxi transporting Einstein slowed just enough at the refueling station to allow Einstein to jump from the moving vehicle before continuing on its way to Chelsea.

Maddox Dayton called his plane Gem. As the last survivor of thirteen planes that had been manufactured for use by the Royal Naval Air Service and Royal Flying Corps between 1912 and 1915, Mayday's plane was indeed as rare as a gem. Built as a trainer, it featured a front cockpit with space enough for two passengers. The aft cockpit was reserved for the pilot. The double forward cockpit also had a full set of controls and was spacious enough to comfortably allow plenty of conversation between Einstein and me over the next few hours. From time to time Mayday would spot an aerodrome at which we would land, refuel, and then be on our way again.

"You said I emigrated to America."

"Yes, that's right. Moriarty had the whole story."

"Where in America did I settle?"

"New Jersey," I replied.

"What is in New Jersey?"

I shook my head. "I have no idea."

Below us the verdant green fields of England lay. It was a land filled with so much history, so much beauty, and so much war. As we flew on to Scotland, my sense was we had an appointment with an enemy far more dangerous than any our tiny nation had ever encountered before.

Suddenly a rat-tat-tat turned our peaceful flight to chaos. A fusillade of bullets tore into the plane. Somewhere behind us, another plane had us in its sights. In an instant we were in a dive streaking toward the earth. As best I could, I turned to look behind me. Mayday was covered with blood, slumped over the controls. He wasn't moving.

"Good heavens, he's been shot!" I cried above the terrible whine of the diving plane.

Einstein turned deathly pale. "Is he dead?"

"I can't tell."

I grabbed the front controls and tried to pull back, but the lifeless pilot was pushing against the controls from behind.

"He has jammed the controls. You will have to push him back," I said to Einstein.

"What?" Einstein asked, horrified.

"You will have to get out and crawl back."

"I can't do that!"

"Can you fly a plane, Professor?"

"No!"

"Then you have no choice. You have to get him off those controls. We haven't much time. Don't think about what you are doing."

Einstein mumbled something in German and climbed unsteadily out the cockpit. I prayed that he wouldn't be blown away. Above us the plane that had shot at us circled lazily and turned back in the direction from which it came. It had done its job.

"Einstein, you really must hurry," I screamed above the deafening whine of the diving plane.

"I am trying," he said, holding onto the wing rigging with one hand and attempting to move our lifeless pilot with the other.

Suddenly the tension in the stick released, allowing me to pull back and gradually bring the plane out of her dive. Einstein slid back into the seat beside me, looking more than a little shocked and slightly exhilarated.

"Well done, Professor."

"You are a pilot, Doctor?"

"No."

Einstein's hand flew to his chest.

"I did receive some fundamental training during the war."

"Enough to get us on the ground?"

"Oh, we'll get on the ground all right. Just pray it's in one piece."

After Einstein had fully recovered himself, he said, "By the way, I found this tucked in the pilot's belt."

Einstein held up an army issue pistol.

"Do you know how to use that thing, Professor?"

"I am not, as the Americans say, a complete chicken egg. I have other skills."

"I believe you must mean egghead. Good show, Professor. Be prepared to use it. One doesn't start a fight with John Watson without John Watson fighting back."

Unbeknownst to our pursuer, who was flying leisurely in an effort to conserve fuel, he was now the pursued. In no time at all the much faster Sopwith caught up to the plane that had attempted to shoot us down. Einstein broke open the pistol to make sure it had a full round of bullets. Approaching from above and behind, I dropped Gem along side our target. The pilot turned to look at us. His mouth visibly sagged open. Einstein and I waved. Then Einstein fired off all six rounds in rapid succession, not at the pilot, but at the engine compartment. Immediately oil and smoke spewed from the plane, its engine sputtering. The plane went into a steep dive. As our antagonist dropped from sight, Einstein and I turned back and headed north once again.

In looking back, our plan had been ill conceived. Moriarty wanted both Holmes and me out of the way. It should have occurred to me that I wasn't safe anywhere. As far as our pursuer knew, I was flying alone. It was a mistake on my part to have risked Einstein's life that way. Had he been killed, I cannot imagine what the consequences should have been. I should have insisted he remain in London.

CHAPTER 17
Return to the Portal

Despite what appeared at first to be a considerable loss of blood, Maddox Dayton's wound had not proved fatal. He was still alive, but unconscious. We made an abrupt landing in a meadow not far from the portal. There I proceeded to treat his injury thanks to an on board medical kit with all the necessaries that allowed me to treat him as if he had come to my surgery. "Will I live?" Dayton asked, after coming round.

"Your wound is serious, but not life threatening. When the anesthetic wears off, you will feel it."

"It's pretty damn sore now. But I think I'm good to fly. I can do this with one hand, you know. They don't call me Mayday for nothing."

"Let's give it a rest for a while. We have some business to attend to. Hopefully it won't take more than an hour. I'll pay you a generous bonus if you will wait."

Dayton was agreeable and Einstein and I proceeded to make our way to the station. Other than the ticket agent inside and a porter, the station was empty. The vagabond I had become accustomed to seeing on the bench was nowhere to be seen. I led Einstein through the station to the end of the platform.

"Is this it?" Einstein asked.

"No." I pointed to the thicket a few meters away. "Beyond is a clearing."

A moment later Holmes pushed his way out of the thicket.

"Holmes!" I cried.

"Watson! Hello, Professor."

"Mr. Holmes, nice to see you again."

The two men shook hands enthusiastically.

"Thank goodness. We understood you had been apprehended by Moriarty."

"Then you did encounter Miss Erikson."

"Yes."

"How is the delightful Miss Erikson?"

"Lately lamented, unfortunately."

"Indeed."

"How were you able to escape, Mr. Holmes?"

"Courtesy of your future self. You were kind enough to provide me with an escape route seconds before Professor Moriarty arrived."

"You and I have become allies in the future?"

"Not quite, Professor. I am afraid you didn't believe a word I said. Your loyalty to Germany is admirable, if not misguided."

"But if I helped you escape—"

"A token of respect regarding our previous acquaintance. This way, Professor."

Holmes led Einstein and me through the thicket into the clearing.

If a man could be filled with wonder then that was Einstein staring up at the two huge stones looming above us. That he could reach out and physically touch what for years had only been theory filled him with awe. "I can hardly believe it is real."

"I assure you it is, Professor."

"I must tell you, Mr. Holmes, there is something most humbling about the realization that a theory has become fact. I feel almost the fool for doubting you."

"Not a fool. We all face a healthy skepticism when faced with things that contradict our previous experiences. We construct theories, and yet we have a difficult time believing in them. The mind is not a vessel to be filled, but a fire to be kindled."

"Plutarch, Mr. Holmes. It is one of my favorite quotes. Tell me how I may be of service. What must we do to dissuade my other self from doing the devil's work? Shall I accompany you and Dr. Watson to Berlin?"

"That had been my thought, but now I believe it might be a mistake."

"It would be, Holmes. There is something the Professor recently shared with me that we must consider. It is called The Exclusion Principle. Two objects from different times cannot occupy the same space at the same time. To do so could be disastrous."

Einstein gave a nod of admiration. "Nicely explained, Doctor. Recall, it is only a theory."

"The portal was only a theory until Wells discovered it." I replied. "Can we afford to take that chance, Professor?"

"Dr. Watson is right," Holmes said. "You are an important man, Professor. The risk is too great. I think you must return to London immediately and book passage on the next steamer to America."

"Holmes, can that make a difference now?"

"Hard to say, Watson. But I think we have no choice. We have no idea what impact our actions in the present have on the future. There is little that is certain. What we know at the moment is the fate of the free world appears to hang in the balance."

"You task me with a profound responsibility, Mr. Holmes."

"If my understanding of the potential of atomic power is correct, that responsibility will extend well beyond the conclusion of the war."

"At the moment atomic research is in its infancy. But scientific knowledge evolves quickly. As each domino falls a momentum builds."

"An apt analogy, Professor. I fear what may be unleashed in the future will result in a domino effect from which there will be no return."

"Then we must hope there is still time to tip the balance in favor of those who stand for freedom." I said.

"Gentlemen, I have been so focused on future events, I have failed to devote much attention to the present. It is reasonable to assume Moriarty has been traveling to and from Germany, or at least passing on information to the Germans, for two, possibly three years."

"I think I have no choice. I will do as you ask, Mr. Holmes. I will abort my plans to return to Germany and notify Mrs. Einstein that we will be vacationing in America."

Holmes glanced at his watch. "The train from Edinburg should arrive in less than an hour."

"We have a plane." I said. "I asked the pilot to stay for a bit."

"Excellent thinking, Doctor."

"Good luck, Professor." Holmes and Einstein shook hands.

Einstein turned to me. "It has been quite the day, Doctor."

"Indeed. God speed," I said, enthusiastically shaking the Professor's hand.

"One last thing, Professor. Would you provide me with some personal article that only you would possess? I am not sure why, but my sense is it could prove invaluable."

Einstein patted his pockets and produced a pocket watch. "This is all I have. You will return it?"

"On my oath."

"It is engraved on the back. E=MC2."

We all had a good chuckle and then Einstein was off, sprinting toward the meadow and the waiting biplane. Holmes and I watched until we were satisfied Einstein was on his way and out of danger before plotting our next steps.

"Holmes, all this jumping back and forth in time is not only exhausting, is it really getting us anywhere? We know Moriarty has steered Einstein into helping the Germans develop this horrible weapon, but it seems all we are doing is playing catch up. How do we get ahead in the game?"

Holmes seemed not to have heard a word I said. He had drifted away, consumed with his own thoughts. "Think, Holmes, think!" He said to himself, pacing erratically. Then he stopped suddenly. "What did you say?"

"I said all we are doing is playing catch up."

"And then you asked, 'How do we get ahead in the game?'"

"Yes."

"That is what we are missing, Watson. Something that will play to our advantage." He pressed his hands against his head and began to pace again. Inadvertently he kicked a stone that ricocheted off one stone and hit another. Holmes considered the stone for a moment, bent down, and then picked it up. He held it out in his hand and let the stone fall. He picked up the stone again, raised his hand higher and let the stone drop once more. "Wells," he said to himself.

"Wells? H.G. Wells? What about Wells?"

"We must stop Einstein from boarding that plane. Quick, Watson!"

Holmes bolted off in the direction of the meadow. I did my best to keep up, but Holmes' long, lanky legs easily outpaced me.

When we arrived at the meadow, the plane was not where it had come to rest. We looked skyward, but there was no plane in sight. It appeared we were too late. But then from the far end of the meadow came the sound of an engine. The plane had taxied down the field in preparation for take off. As the plane came toward us, Holmes ran into its path waving his arms. As the wheels lifted off the ground, the pilot spotted Holmes and quickly pulled back on the throttle. The plane dropped erratically back onto the meadow and turned back toward us. Holmes approached the waiting plane. Maddox Dayton and Einstein were seated together in the forward cockpit.

"Sorry, old chap," Holmes, said to the pilot. "I have a question for Professor Einstein."

"Are you sure you're able to pilot this plane?" I asked of Maddox Dayton. The landing was terribly handled.

"He's the one flying," Dayton said, pointing to Einstein.

Einstein shrugged. "What is it, Mr. Holmes?" He hollered over the roar of the engine.

"Professor, if I understand Newton's second law of motion, a falling object accelerates due to the force of gravity acting upon it."

"Yes, that is correct," Einstein replied.

"Can the same be said of time? Does time accelerate in a wormhole?"

"Very good, Mr. Holmes. Excellent question. Theoretically time does accelerate. It is referred to as time dilation."

"By way of example, what might the time dilation be for a wormhole that comes out eighteen years in the future?"

"We are speaking of hypotheticals. It is impossible to say. It could be a matter of hours or days. We have no way to make that determination."

"Thank you, Professor," Holmes yelled. "Have a safe journey. Give our regards to America."

Following Mayday's directions, Einstein turned the plane around, revved the engine, and sped down the meadow, precariously lifting off for London.

"What happened to the pilot?" Holmes asked.

"It's a long story. What was that all about Newton's second law?"

"It may be the break we've needed."

"Explain."

"You remember our conversation with Wells. He said there was something about that calendar in the German tavern that he could not put his finger on. He was so distracted by the year, he didn't pay much attention to the date."

"If I recall, he said the month and day were the same. He left on a Wednesday and he arrived on Wednesday."

"But the date, Watson. The date. There was something about those X's through the expired days. What if Wells arrived on a Wednesday a week later?"

"You've been through the portal twice, and I once. We checked into the hotel and signed the guest register. Wouldn't we have noticed?"

"We had other things on our minds. It wouldn't occur to us. Even if we had seen a date, it may not have registered."

"If that is the case, what importance may we attach to it?"

"I have been so busy trying to piece together the larger picture I have failed to consider the small. I have an idea, but it will require our returning to Berlin."

"Holmes, is that wise? Aren't we putting ourselves in danger? We have no allies in Berlin."

"Whatever move Moriarty plans to make against us, it will be here in our own time, it won't be in the future. Moriarty knows there are too many unknowns."

"Wouldn't it make more sense to apprehend him here and put an end to all of this?"

"Not until we know the full extent of Moriarty's plans. It is impossible to know what damage he has already done. He has had a three years head start. We have no way of knowing how much British intelligence has already been compromised. Clearly he is not communicating with and traveling to Germany by conventional means. He has a network. We must discover it and crush it, otherwise it will live on without him."

Reluctantly I followed Holmes to the clearing once again and reentered the portal. Eighteen years and one week later, we were in Berlin once again.

CHAPTER 18
Loomings

A light rain was falling when Holmes and I stepped into the alley. Low dark clouds hung over Berlin casting the city in a dull gray pall.

Holmes assured me we would be safe at The Blue House, but I couldn't but feel apprehensive. Darden Poppin had betrayed us. Why shouldn't the proprietors of The Blue House betray us as well?

"Watson, Moriarty knows, as well as we, we have no allies here. There are no authorities we can go to. He is safe, and we are safe.

"We are safe until the moment we return to England."

"We shall deal with that eventuality in due time."

Max Veidt greeted us warmly. I tried to detect some undercurrent of duplicity in the proprietor's demeanor, but he gave away nothing. He was either a seasoned professional, or perhaps he did not care. Or perhaps he did not know, Holmes suggested. I seriously doubted that, as it had been Darden Poppin who had led us to The Blue House. I felt as if I were playing chess wearing a blindfold. One move felt as random and pointless as the next.

Upon signing the guest register, both Holmes and I noted the date. It was as Holmes guessed, a week later.

The following morning after a hearty breakfast, Holmes allowed he would spend the day at the Berlin State Library. It was a repository for the world's major newspapers.

I hoped we had returned to Berlin for matters more important than reading newspapers. "What do you expect to learn?" I asked.

"Impossible to say."

Throughout the years, I had become accustomed to Holmes' certitude to the point of his becoming annoying. This adventure had me quite out of sorts. Of late everything seemed to be vague, uncertain, inconclusive. Most unlike Holmes.

"Very well," I said. I had no desire to go to the library. "I will look for you this evening then."

"I will join you for a drink in the lounge later."

Holmes set off for the library and I returned to my room, settling into a comfortable armchair. I felt both weary and restless. I should have liked to read, but fatigue overcame me and I fell asleep where I sat.

The Berlin State library was established in 1661. Throughout its long history, it had faced many challenges: economic turmoil, war, meddling kings and queens, and the Nazis. Despite its ups and downs, the library featured some of the world's most treasured works. Among them were a copy of the Gutenberg Bible, a third century Coptic codex of the Book of Proverbs, symphonies by Bach and Beethoven and several operas by Mozart, not to mention hundreds of other priceless works. When the Nazis seized power, they methodically set about eliminating anyone and anything that might undermine Nazi doctrine. Books and people disappeared by the thousands. Invaluable works were torched. The Nazi vision was singular. Nothing was spared that did not support their aims. Enemies were one thing, but books were far more of a threat. Ideas lived on. Remarkably, the library survived, retaining its status as one of the most important libraries in the world.

As was his modus operandi, Holmes entered the library as if he had been there dozens of times before. Nothing was quite so off putting as someone who exuded confidence and authority to the point of intimidation, a quality many Germans fully appreciated. When asked by a library staff member if she could offer assistance, Holmes simply glared at the woman to the point of discomfort and promptly ignored her. He had no difficulty finding the periodical area. Given what he knew of the library's reputation, he felt sure he would find an ample collection of the world's most important newspapers. He was only slightly disappointed.

Holmes spent several hours scanning current issues of the various Nazi propaganda dailies. He read German well enough to comprehend the direction Germany was moving. The papers were filled with despicable stories about Jews, communists, liberals, homosexuals, gypsies, and the disabled. They promoted an agenda of racial purity and sang the praises of Hitler and the goals of National Socialism. By the time he had finished reading the German papers, he felt quite sickened. The little he had learned from Darden Poppin and what Moriarty had revealed was nothing compared to what he was now discovering on his own. His earlier pronouncements of threats to the freedom of the world now seemed pale by comparison. This threat wasn't new. It had been building for years almost completely ignored. It was inconceivable to Holmes that a British prime minister could have so misjudged what was happening in Germany to the point of calling for a policy of appeasement.

As he expected, there was no mention of Germany's atomic program. That was top secret. But there was more to it than that. It was more than the atomic bomb. Germany was bent on something that would endure a century, perhaps even longer. It had to be stopped now and in the past. If necessary, Holmes was prepared to give his own life to ensure that whatever Germany was building would be destroyed permanently.

He returned the Nazi propaganda papers to their proper places on the shelves and visited the men's room to wash his hands. After a thorough wash up, he still felt soiled by what he had handled.

Next he turned his attention to the English language papers. In particular he wanted *The London Times*. It came as no surprise that the most recent copy was seven years old. Holmes had no doubt Nazi officials themselves received *The Times* daily, but ordinary citizens were not afforded the luxury of information that was not heavily filtered through the propaganda machines of Joseph Goebbels.

Holmes began with the most recent volumes and worked backwards, quickly scanning the deaths of famous writers and painters, skirmishes here and there, pacts, treaties, natural and man made tragedies. Two things unsettled Holmes. The first was what he considered a blind eye to events taking place in Germany. He detected little cause for concern. Perhaps because he was viewing events after they had happened, his perspective provided him with a view impossible for others to entertain. The second event that shook him concerned the aftermath of October 29, 1929. Economies worldwide had collapsed and ruined lives. The effects had lasted years. So much heartache and devastation had resulted. What, if anything, could he do? What, if anything, should he do?

Overhead a loud speaker crackled. "Die Bibliothek schliest in einer Stunde." Holmes reached into his pocket and pulled out Einstein's watch. It was five o'clock. He needed to be finished by six.

After scanning numerous volumes of *The London Times*, Holmes arrived at the issues dated 1921. As he rapidly thumbed through the newspapers, one headline commanded his attention. His heart stopped and his blood froze.

Bizarre Coincidence
Claims Lives of Sherlock Holmes and Dr. Watson

In what authorities are describing as a bizarre coincidence, the detective   Sherlock   Holmes   and   his associate Dr. John H. Watson were killed in separate incidents only hours apart.

At the request of the Norfolk police, Inspector Lestrade of Scotland Yard is assisting the investigation. As of this writing details are not entirely clear; however, first reports indicate the internationally known detective was involved in a scheme to provide top-secret documents to a foreign power.

According to authorities, Major Darden Poppin was forced to fatally wound the   world   famous   detective   in defense of his own life. The incident occurred in a coastal village in Norfolk.

In a separate incident, John H. Watson was killed in a car crash a few miles northwest of Cromer. It is believed Dr. Watson's car skidded into the opposite lane and crashed through the railing of the bluff along the seacoast road. Dr. Watson had dined at the Hotel de Paris earlier that evening with a female companion.

All indications suggest the accident was weather related.

Holmes quickly scanned subsequent issues for additional details. For reasons not entirely clear to him, there was no mention of the village in which the incident had taken place. He took a deep breath and steepled his fingers together so his thumbs pressed against his chin and the tips of his fingers against his forehead. Anyone observing him might have thought he was deep in prayer.

This was not the first time Holmes had read his own obituary. Papers the world over had covered his celebrated death at Reichenbach Falls. The essential difference being that then Holmes read his obituary after the fact. Now he was reading his obituary before his death was to occur.

While Holmes spent the day at the library, I spent an ample portion of my afternoon sleeping. That was an indulgence I rarely afforded myself. Finally guilt got the better of me. I was determined to salvage the rest of the day, despite feeling groggier than I had before embarking on my afternoon-long snooze. With no way of knowing when Holmes would return, I bathed and dressed and went down to the lounge. I took a seat inside overlooking the nicely kept garden below the terrace. Admittedly it wasn't as ornate as an English garden, but it was commendable. Max was my waiter. The Blue House seemed to have no employees except the owners

"What do you recommend, Max?" I tried to conduct myself in the most congenial manner, but I must admit to more than a slight prejudice concerning our host.

"Are you a Scotch drinker, Dr. Watson?"

"I am," I said. "What do you have?"

"Dalmore. 1920. What do you say to that?"

My first thought was no. A Scotch that young hadn't even begun the aging process. Then I had to remind myself this was 1939. "Let's give it a try," I said.

"How do you like it? With a splash of water?"

"Neat."

"Coming right up."

Max went behind the bar and poured the whisky. It occurred to me that Max might try to poison me. Had Holmes been in my presence he would have assured me that would not be the case. That he could be so resolute was irksome. I, on the other hand, always maintained a healthy doubt.

"Excuse me," a pleasing voice said from behind.

My conflicting thoughts about Max came to a sudden end. I turned to see who was addressing me. A strikingly attractive middle-aged lady was standing nearby.

"I don't mean to interrupt, but you are Dr. Watson, are you not?"

I rose from my chair. Instinctively I took a quick glance about the room. Recent events had made me skittish about the sudden approach of strangers. "Yes, I am," I said, offering my hand.

"Lurlene Haas," the woman said, slipping her warm hand into mine. "I recognize you from photographs I have often seen in newspapers. I am quite the fan of your writing."

"That is most kind of you. I was just about to have a drink. Would you care to join me?"

"I couldn't impose, really."

"Not an imposition at all. I would appreciate the company."

"Very well."

I pulled out another chair for my guest. Max returned to the table with my Scotch. "What may I get for the lady?" Max asked.

"A martini please. Gin."

"Of course." Max returned to the bar.

"If I may be so candid, Doctor, I must say I am surprised. I wouldn't have expected someone of your stature to be in Berlin, not these days."

"I am more than a little surprised myself, Mrs. Haas."

"It's Miss. But please, call me Annalise. I much prefer it to Lurlene."

"Annalise it is. I go by John."

"A man of your reputation, that may be difficult for me. But I will do my best."

Max returned with the martini.

"To what shall we toast?" I asked.

"Good fortune? Happy coincidences? New friends?"

"To new friends," I said, tapping my glass against hers. "What brings you to The Blue House, Annalise?"

"I write for a travel magazine, *Here and There*. I try to write interesting stories about interesting places."

"Interesting."

We both laughed at the silliness of my response.

"I love to travel and to write about my experiences, but I am afraid it has become a challenge. With Europe teetering on the brink of war, it is becoming too dangerous. Frankly, reading travel articles is not uppermost in the minds of most people these days. The magazine trade is in dire straits."

"One can hope for the best."

"What about you, Doctor? Correction, John."

"Oh! I am here on a little travel adventure," I replied, sounding anything but convincing.

"That was rude of me," Annalise said apologetically. "I put you on the spot. That was not my intent."

"No, no, not at all."

In the window in front of me, I saw Holmes' reflection. I turned to look over my shoulder, but Holmes had already stepped away from the entrance to the lounge.

"Perhaps we could have dinner together this evening," I suggested with uncharacteristic boldness. "That is if you are free."

"I would like that very much. Shall we say eight o'clock?"

"Eight o'clock then." I rose from my chair and exited the lounge.

Holmes was waiting for me in the lobby.

"Why so furtive?" I asked.

"I didn't wish to impose."

"It wouldn't have been an imposition at all," I replied. "The lady and I are meeting for dinner. Her name is Lurlene Haas."

"You don't say," Holmes responded in rather an odd manner.

"She prefers to be called Annalise." I tried to gauge Holmes' response. Was it disinterest or something else? "Is something the matter?"

"It occurs to me Lurlene is German for temptress."

"I will keep that in mind." We ascended the stairs to Holmes' room, which was adjacent to mine.

"Drink?" Holmes asked as he went to directly to the terrace.

I waved off his offer. "I have just had one. How was your visit to the library?" I followed him onto the terrace.

"I have spent most of my day reading current and old newspapers."

"What have you learned?"

"I am afraid we have grossly underestimated this coming war."

"You speak of it as if it were a certainty."

"It is a certainty, Watson. There can be no doubt about that. There is a lunacy at work in this country unlike anything I have ever witnessed. The local papers are filled with a rabid nationalism that should frankly worry the rest of the world."

"There you've said it yourself, Holmes. Nationalism. Is that so unusual after a nation has suffered an ignominious defeat in war? Isn't that the natural state to rally the people in order to rebuild? It takes years, decades for a nation to recover."

"That is precisely the calculus the rest of the world is missing. This country is at full strength now, Watson, and it has accomplished that feat in a remarkably short period of time. With the help of Moriarty and Einstein, Germany is building a formidable war machine. I can assure you, the nations of the world fighting side by side will be no match."

"Holmes, we are doing what we can. Isn't that why we are here?"

"John, you know me well. It isn't enough. We must do more."

In my long association with Sherlock Holmes there have only been a few times when he has called me by my given name. It has either been in a time of extreme crisis or a moment of unusual sentiment. In this case it was both.

"I am afraid we are no closer now to thwarting Germany's plans than we were when we began this enterprise."

"Holmes, this is unusual for you. You are surely not admitting defeat."

"No. It is something else. You are quite taken with Miss Haas, are you not?"

"We have only just met, but, yes, I look forward to seeing her this evening. We had a pleasant time."

"Would it surprise you to learn you have met Miss Haas before?"

"Holmes, I can't think what you are getting at. We have never met. Such a striking woman, I would certainly remember."

"In our own time you haven't met Miss Haas yet, but you will. The outcome will not be pleasant."

"Good lord, Holmes, you are not making sense. I think you must lie down. You must be suffering from exhaustion."

"My afternoon in the library allowed me a great deal of time to look through newspapers present and past. I came across an article in *The London Times* dated five days from now in 1921. You will meet Miss Haas in London and spend two glorious days with her. And then, inexplicably, you will lose your life in a car crash in what I presume is a vain attempt to rescue me before I am shot to death by a British agent. The case will generate sensational headlines worldwide. Lestrade will be called to assist with the investigation. A futile attempt will be made to link the two incidents. In spite of conspiracy theories by fans and skeptics, the investigation will prove inconclusive and will be written off as a coincidence worthy of pulp magazines. The upshot will be that I will be accused of treason, and you will be implicated as a co-conspirator. Our reputations will be blackened forever."

"It is hard for me to believe. Where does this take place?"

"In Norfolk. In none of the articles is the village ever identified."

"That's unusual. You would think that is common knowledge. Why keep a location secret, unless there is some other importance attached to it. Who has the power to censor *The London Times*?"

"Indeed."

"What about the agent? Is he identified?"

"Darden Poppin. The same Darden Poppin who befriended us in Berlin and then betrayed us."

"Holmes, good Lord! How can that be? Had you met Poppin prior to your encounter at the Berlin Train Station?"

"No, at least not yet. But he had met me."

"I am not following."

"Recall Watson, the time dilation. We are seven days ahead. The reason we cannot recall Darden Poppin and Miss Haas is because we have yet to meet them. We will meet them this week. We have been caught up in a complex game both here and in the past. Since that fortuitous meeting with Darden Poppin in the train station, I have felt uneasy. Our encounter was too convenient. Reading those accounts in *The Times* allowed me to see a much larger picture. I came to the unsettling realization that we have not been on an equal footing in this contest with Professor Moriarty. In fact we have not been participants in this game at all, Watson."

"How so, Holmes?"

"I am afraid my arrogance and pride have led to my being played the fool. I have vastly underestimated Moriarty to what may be a disastrous degree."

It was a rare admission that Holmes owned up to a misjudgment.

"Moriarty has had a three years head start on us. He has had more than enough time to read the same papers as I and to make his plans. You and I have been competing on a table tennis top. Moriarty's field of play has been the world. He has anticipated our every move. We have been pawns. He has hedged his bets beautifully both in the past and the present."

If Holmes were right, we were involved in something that far exceeded our abilities to fully understand or control. "How do we proceed?" I asked. "If Moriarty is influencing events both past and present, how can we thwart him? It is daunting, Holmes, daunting, not to mention we are now on borrowed time. Knowing my fate is wholly unsettling. I am at a complete loss as to know how to proceed."

"Watson, you are not going to be killed in a car crash and I am certainly not going to allow Darden Poppin to gun me down."

"But Holmes, you said yourself, you read those stories in *The London Times*."

"We mustn't lose sight of the fact that the portal has sent us into the future eighteen years and seven days. Our reality remains 1921. This present--this future in 1939--can only be based upon what happens in the past. In one sense, it doesn't actually exist. What happens here is entirely dependent on what will have already happened. Should you and I meet our demise, then that is it. Nothing in our past can be undone. It is the actions we have yet to take that will be the ones that influence future events. It is those seven days that are so crucial, Watson. Knowing what will happen in the immediate seven days gives us the advantage we have been looking for."

"Holmes, can we really escape our fate?"

"I don't believe there is a path decided for us in advance, Watson. And I certainly don't give a damn about what is written in a future edition of *The London Times*."

I couldn't recall when I had heard Holmes swear.

"*The Times* reports what has happened. It does not predict what will happen. We have the ability to control our lives, Watson, and that is what we will do."

"What baffles me is Miss Haas acted as if we had never met before."

"In 1921 you haven't met yet."

"I understand that, but you would think she would have remarked that I had hardly seemed to have aged from the photographs she claimed to have recognized me from."

"She is working for Moriarty. She knows you have traveled from the past. It is a seemingly insignificant mistake that speaks volumes. It is a mistake Poppin avoided. He explicitly noted I seemed not to have aged."

"Are Poppin and Miss Haas assassins?"

"No, I believe their main purpose is to keep us under surveillance. Moriarty cannot take the chance of such a disruption to time, certainly not here in the future. Whatever lies in store for us must play out in our own time. Poppin and Miss Haas are quite aware that you and I will have our appointments with destiny within the next few days."

"Those stories you read in the papers, they were printed and tangible. What happens to those newspapers if the events that have already been reported don't occur?"

Holmes pondered my question for a very long time. Finally he said, "I have no idea, Watson, nor do I care. You and I are concerned with but one reality, and that is the one we must protect and return to immediately."

"It is unfortunate, I rather fancy Miss Haas, you know. Pity she's a spy."

"If Moriarty has not already met Miss Haas in 1921, you can easily upset his plans by meeting her first."

"Won't that be like looking for a needle in a haystack?"

"Not at all. She is an Austrian national traveling on a passport, which requires a local address. Not to mention that she writes for a well-known travel magazine. I see no reason why you shouldn't be able to find her. If all else fails, we will ask Mycroft to intercede. As it is, we must pay him a visit."

"Holmes, this business with Poppin has got me stumped. How could he have known when you would be at the station?"

"Informants, no doubt. I suspect Moriarty has operatives on the street near the alley where the portal is located. As soon as I was observed, a call would have been placed to Poppin."

"Wouldn't that risk giving away the location of the portal?"

"Which is why the operatives would be stationed on the street and not in the alley. Individuals suddenly appearing in a dead-end alley would attract no end of attention."

"How could Moriarty be sure you would go to the station?"

"A reasonable guess. What better place for an individual to lose himself than in a bustling station teeming with travelers? Should I have gone elsewhere, Moriarty's operatives would have instructed Poppin otherwise. We have been under continual surveillance."

Holmes and I checked out of The Blue House and returned to the portal. Fortunately for the operative posted near the alley, he was asleep. As such there was no need to assault him. Holmes and I slipped into the portal and instantly reappeared in Scotland.

The moment we approached the station, our friendly extortionist greeted us. "One pound, please." At his feet was one of Moriarty's henchmen. The fellow was bound and gagged.

"Pay him, Watson."

"Here," I said. "It is good to know you're on the right side."

"I don't take sides, I just take money." He gave the man laying on the ground a good kick in the side. The man grunted painfully through his gag. "He wouldn't pay."

Holmes and I made our way down the station platform.

"What should I do with him?" The vagrant asked.

"Not our concern," Holmes said.

"Right." The vagrant gave us a thumbs up and dragged the poor fellow off the platform and into the bushes.

An hour later The Royal Scot from Edinburg to London shunted into Loch Naire Station. Holmes and I boarded and had a compartment to ourselves. We had little to say. I think we were both overwhelmed by what we knew of the future and what needed to be done. The journey was a pleasant but brief respite from what was to come.

Whatever became of the chap bound and gagged is anyone's guess.

CHAPTER 19
Mycroft Holmes

Mycroft Holmes. Now there's one for the ages. Holmes' older brother. The cliché has yet to be written that can adequately describe the relationship between these two and their similarities and dissimilarities. Suffice to say that Mycroft had a slight edge on his younger brother with regard to intelligence, very slight.

As co-founder, Mycroft Holmes was a frequent visitor to London's exclusive Diogenes Club. It was here men of social, economic, and political importance gathered to ignore each other. Nary a word was spoken in the Diogenes Club. Any offense resulted in a reprimand and multiple offenses would result in one being permanently barred. It was a gathering place filled with comfortable chairs and a variety of periodicals for those who did not wish to engage in conversation and expected absolute quiet. In short it was similar to a library for the stuffy. The club itself had no appeal for me. I actually preferred the company of others, and frankly wished I were presently in the company of Miss Haas.

I have never been able to report with any accuracy Mycroft's role in the British government. His position still remains illusive. Suffice to say he is an important man with important responsibilities whatever they may be. Holmes and I made our way to Mycroft's favorite location. He was reading a newspaper and quite aware that Sherlock and I were standing in front of him. Seeing as he had no intention of acknowledging us, I cleared my throat. I might as well have burst into an operatic aria. Papers rustled and glaring looks shot as arrows toward me. Mycroft folded his paper and pursed his lips. Sherlock nodded his head in the direction of The

Stranger's Room. It was the only room in the Diogenes Club in which one could converse. I followed Holmes and his brother into the handsomely appointed room and closed the door. We were its only occupants.

"What is it?" Mycroft asked without greeting either of us.

It had been some time since I had last seen Mycroft. I am pleased to report his physical appearance had improved considerably. For far too long he had been grossly overweight and lethargic. Years of overindulging in food and drink had taken its toll. Perhaps coming to terms with early mortality brought about a change. It was clear he was now regulating his diet and taking exercise.

"Thank you," said Holmes. "It is nice to see you as well. I commend you on your efforts to exert a measure of control over your life."

"Thank you, it hasn't been easy. As I am limiting my club visits to twice a week, I must insist that you get on with it." Mycroft acknowledged my presence for the first time since we had arrived. "John, good to see you."

I smiled politely.

"I assume you are here about a case." Mycroft gestured for us to sit.

The chairs were exceedingly comfortable. I would look into obtaining one of my own.

"I am involved in a case that has far reaching implications for the security of our nation well beyond our borders and well into the future."

"No one may accuse Sherlock Holmes of understatement," Mycroft replied with undisguised cynicism.

"I am not at liberty to provide you with all the details. John will vouch for me. England is under considerable threat."

I was certain Holmes would not divulge the existence of the portal. Whether in the hands of an enemy or our own government, well-intentioned men invariably find ways to pervert scientific discoveries that should otherwise be used for good.

"What is it you want of me?"

"Your help in locating a German agent by the name of Darden Poppin."

"I have never heard of the man."

"This man poses a great danger to the security of England."

"As I said—'

"You are misled into believing Poppin is a double agent. He has been educated and trained here in England, but he is not loyal to the crown. I assure you his allegiance is to Germany."

"Brother, after its humiliating defeat, Germany poses no credible threat."

"If you believed that, you wouldn't have an agent in place, albeit a double agent whose loyalties you have grossly misunderstood."

"I have no idea what you are talking about."

"What you cannot anticipate, Mycroft, is how far reaching Germany's plans are."

"Sherlock, whatever you think you may know, you are dancing precariously close to matters that are top secret. My ability to protect you goes only so far."

"We will take our chances. There is far more at stake here than you realize or can conceive."

"British intelligence is second to none. We are monitoring the Germans very carefully. They are in no position to declare war. They are in no position to do anything."

"The Germans are developing an atomic weapon

that could result in the complete annihilation of its enemies."

Mycroft smiled sardonically. "The hyperbole continues."

"The work is being directed by Moriarty."

Mycroft frowned. "Dear departed Professor Moriarty, your favorite nemesis. I should have known." Mycroft leaned forward to rise from his chair. "Thank you, gentlemen. You have been most entertaining."

Holmes leaned forward, put a hand on his brother's shoulder, and gently pushed him back into his chair. The cushion beneath Mycroft sighed.

"Mycroft, ignorance and arrogance are not becoming of a man in your position. As improbable as it seems, Moriarty is alive. He has been in Germany for the past three years helping the Germans develop a weapon that will most assuredly be used in the coming world war."

"The coming war?"

"A war that will be unlike all others, and one that England will not win this time."

"May we dispense with the theatrics?"

"You should listen to your brother," I said.

"You believe Moriarty survived Reichenbach?"

"That should be the least of your concerns. What I can tell you is Darden Poppin is a key player. It is imperative we locate him."

"You are familiar with the British Secrets Act?"

"Of course."

"Then you have your answer." Mycroft Holmes rose and walked toward the door.

"Then you won't help us," Holmes said with uncharacteristic resignation.

Mycroft stopped short of the door. "Good day,

gentlemen." The piston on the door hissed quietly as Mycroft exited, softly pushing the door closed behind him.

I turned to Holmes. "I am disheartened." We seemed to have hit a brick wall.

"If we do nothing and allow events to unfold naturally, Moriarty will draw us into his snare. Or we can be a step ahead. The sooner we travel to Norfolk, the better."

"Holmes, Norfolk is a large area to cover."

"Remember, old chap, the article said a remote coastal village. Our search need only be confined to the towns along the coast."

"If you ask me, we're going to need a miracle."

Holmes did not believe in miracles. For him the unexpected or the extraordinary were neither matters of luck nor fortune. Thus he couldn't allow himself to utter the word *miracle* when a marvelous bit of good fortune presented itself in the guise of Peter Johns, a farmer from the coastal village of Salthouse.

CHAPTER 20
Randall's Folly

Salthouse lies about one hundred and forty miles north and east of London. It is located in the county of Norfolk. There is little to distinguish Salthouse from dozens of other coastal villages except for a curiosity known as Randall's Folly. Randall was one Onesiphorus Randall, a property developer who had done well for himself in London. Around 1840, Randall set about building a castle for himself on a stretch of beach called The Great Eye. Why there and for what purpose remains unknown. Local historians suggest its purpose may have had something to do with Randall's reputation as a sort of Casanova. The castle most likely served as a destination for his many conquests. Doors on both sides of the structure allowed for the easy entrance and exit of Randall's carriages, which ferried his lovers to and from. Well out of sight of nosy onlookers, a lady could enter and exit Randall's carriage while maintaining the utmost privacy. In time the house fell into disrepair and was subsequently purchased by the local Board of Trade. Its location on the beach made it ideal for what became known as the rocket brigade, a life-saving unit designed to rescue those besieged by the sea. An apparatus used by the rocket brigade eventually lead to locals simply referring to the dilapidated structure as The Rocket House.

For the past several years the house had been abandoned. It was for that reason it attracted the attention of Peter Johns, a local farmer whose own house sat across the road beyond the marshes that separated the small village from the seawall beyond which The Rocket House stood. Except for periods of heavy fog, The

Rocket House was easily visible to Peter Johns from Creek Cottage, the house he shared with the missus. One night as Peter John stood outside smoking his last pipe of the day, as the missus wouldn't allow that filthy thing inside, he glanced across the marshes in the direction of The Rocket House. There he witnessed something he had not seen for many years: a light glowed in one of the windows. He tapped out his pipe on the stonewall that protected his property from the main road. Some of the glowing ash reignited in the breeze that blew in from the sea, sending a shower of sparks like a firework. "Fancy that," the farmer said to himself. "That's unusual." He dug out the last ashes of his pipe and put the incident out of mind. It wasn't even worth mentioning to the missus. The next night he witnessed the light again and the night after that. Now it was time to say something.

The following morning as Constable Robby was making his rounds, Peter Johns waved the jovial policeman toward him. Had he seen? Did he know?

Constable Robby shook his head. From his own place, he couldn't see The Rocket House at night. He did agree it seemed unusual, since nobody had occupied the place for years. He would look into it. Nothing much ever happened in Salthouse and this seemed the sort of thing that jolly well ought to be investigated. In fact Peter Johns thought Constable Robby seemed almost giddy by the prospect of getting to do some actual police work. "I'll look into it," Constable Robby said.

Peter Johns didn't know when the constable's investigation would actually begin, but he was satisfied he had done his part. He had reported something curious and now it was up to the constable to do something about it. In the meantime he had a farm to look after and business in London to take care of. He and the missus would be gone for two days. They would overnight in London with Peter Johns' brother.

Two days later when Peter Johns and the missus arrived home, they were greeted with tragic news. The village was in a state of shock. Constable Robby had been found dead, his lifeless body floating in one of the marsh ponds between the main road and the seawall. It was impossible to explain. How had this happened? Constable Robby knew the village as well as any man. He could never have been so careless as to fall into a marsh pond at night. Had he been drinking? The constable was not a drinker. Had it been deliberate? He was a dedicated family man without so much as a care. Could it have been murder? Why? Constable Robby didn't have an enemy in the world. Or did he, Peter Johns thought to himself. Had the constable investigated the light in The Rocket House while Peter Johns and the missus were away in London? It might not be safe to voice his speculations. After all, one couldn't be sure whom to trust. And yet something needed to be done. He would return to London the following week to finalize some documents with the bank. While there he would make it a point to visit the one man in London in whom he felt he could confide. He would again spend the night at his brother's home, but it would not be his brother who would serve as his confidante.

CHAPTER 21
Peter Johns

"And that's it," Peter Johns said. "There's nary another word I can tell you, Mr. Holmes."

"Yes, you were quite right in coming here, Peter. It is good to see you again after so many years." Mycroft Holmes turned to his brother and me. "I will leave you both to it then." On his way out Mycroft and Sherlock Holmes exchanged nods. Nothing more needed to be said. Without revealing any secrets, Mycroft Holmes had given us the break we desperately needed.

Holmes steepled his fingers together in that classic pose that seemed essential to drawing out his thoughts. "Tell me, Mr. Johns, do you walk the beach often?"

Peter Johns seemed at a loss for words. Holmes' question seemed completely irrelevant to the matter at hand.

"I ask," Holmes said, "because I observe a white residue that has stained the leather of your boots. Dried seawater presents such a staining pattern."

"It's true, the missus and I sometimes take walks along the beach."

"I also detect an oily substance. Is that also from the beach?"

"Well, yes. Mr. Holmes, if I should have taken off my boots—"

"No, not at all. I am merely attempting to test a theory. Are there pockets of oil along the beach?"

"Often, but not always."

"If you will allow me." Holmes took a pencil from his brother's desk and bent toward Peter Johns boots." He scraped the pencil across the gooey substance and then passed the pencil under his nose. "As I thought, Watson. Diesel."

"What is the significance of that?" Peter Johns asked.

Holmes offered his hand. "You have been most helpful, Mr. Johns." He opened the door for our guest. "The secretary will see you out."

Before he could collect his thoughts, the door slammed behind Peter Johns and he found himself standing face to face with Mycroft Holmes' secretary. "I don't know what to think," the befuddled farmer said.

"Most people don't," the secretary said, leading Peter Johns downstairs and bidding him a good day.

I stood at the window and looked down on Peter Johns who scratched his head and ambled off down Whitehall. "Dirty boots. I must say I rather hoped we might come away with something more substantial."

"We have, Watson. The man was a trove of information: the abandoned manor, the mysterious death of the constable, and diesel on the man's boots. I am convinced we have discovered the location of Darden Poppin's rendezvous point. U-boats are powered by diesel, which could account for the pockets of oil along the beach. Poppin may well be traveling to and from Germany by way of U-boat."

"As a British agent, why would that be necessary? He certainly has a diplomatic passport. An agent may travel wherever and whenever he chooses."

"Espionage is a complex business."

"Do you believe Mycroft knows of the U-boat?"

"Possibly, which could account for the news blackout on Salthouse. There have been cases in which governments have allowed bombings and ship disasters to occur to protect secrets. Allowing the incursion of the

U-boat may play to some larger purpose."

"However, there is another player."

"Exactly. Quite apart from whatever espionage Poppin is engaged in, his second master is Moriarty. The professor is no doubt traveling to and from Germany by U-boat as well. He is transporting secrets and Poppin is an ally in that undertaking."

"Do you think Poppin had a hand in the constable's murder?"

"Most likely to forestall the constable from digging deeper. Poppin couldn't have anticipated a local farmer would have connections to Whitehall. One may only hope that after hearing Peter Johns' story, Mycroft may be entertaining some doubts about Major Poppin's loyalty."

"Time is running out. What is our next move?"

"I think we must upset the apple cart."

CHAPTER 22
Coming ashore

The man standing guard atop Randall's Folly peered seaward, attempting to see through the fog rolling in from the North Sea. He had heard something. As the guard stared intently into the darkness, a fishing boat drifted through the fog and ran aground on the pebble beach. A moment later a bearded man came out of the small cabin, walked to the bow, and slid over the side to the beach. The guard quickly made his way from the parapet and intercepted the man. "Who goes there?" The guard asked, raising his rifle.

The bearded man wearing a captain's cap and pea coat ignored the guard.

"I said identify yourself," the guard commanded.

"Bugger off," the man said.

The guard approached, shining a torch at the bearded man. "Identify yourself."

The gruff looking man turned. "I'm not looking for trouble. Engine problem. Where's the nearest inn?"

The guard lowered his rifle. "The Nag's Head. Cross the marshes to the high road. You can see the light from here."

"Thankee," the bearded man said.

Watching the stranger disappear into the dark, the guard would report the incident to his superior as soon as possible.

Three quarters of an hour later, the stranger had taken a room at The Nag's Head. He was now nursing a pint at a table in the adjoining pub.

"You're new here," a voice said.

The seaman didn't look up from his mug. "What's it to you?"

"It's a small village."

"I won't be staying long."

"Major Darden Poppin," the small, but muscular man said. He offered his hand in friendship. The stranger ignored the extended hand. "I was traveling from up north to Folkestone. My engine broke down."

"I didn't catch your name," Poppin prodded.

"I didn't give it. If it's any of your business, it's Magwitch. Able Magwitch. Interrogation over?"

"Welcome to Salthouse, Mr. Magwitch. May I buy you another?" Poppin asked, noting the man's nearly empty glass.

"If I wanted company, I would have asked for it. I can afford my own drink."

Poppin acceded to the man's wishes and returned to the table he had been sharing with two other men. Despite appearing to be engaged in conversation, Poppin positioned himself in such a way as to keep an eye on the stranger.

Magwitch finished his pint and turned in for the night.

In the dead of night, Magwitch snapped awake. Something cold and sharp pressed against his throat. He could barely breathe. In the dark a thumbnail scraped against a match. The match ignited, illuminating the face of Darden Poppin. He moved the match to the wick of the kerosene lamp sitting on the bedside table. The room lit up in an orange glow. Poppin was leaning forward in a chair, holding a German knife against the seaman's neck.

"Now, who are you really? Able Magwitch is a character from a novel."

"Every English schoolboy would have recognized that name immediately. That it took you half the night before discovering that says more about you than it says about me."

Poppin withdrew the knife from the old sailor's throat and sat back in his chair. "You first."

The grizzled old seaman threw his legs over the side of the bed. He was still wearing the clothes he had arrived in. "My name is Jack Brewster. I was on my way from Hull to Folkestone. From there I was headed to London. My engine gave up and I put in here."

"No one sent you here?"

"Why would anyone send me to this pimple on a pig's arse? Come daylight you can see for yourself. The engine's completely knackered."

"What business do you have in London?"

"My business, my concern."

Poppin turned the knife so that the light from the lantern reflected off the highly polished steel blade.

Jack Brewster nodded his head. "A man. I owe him something."

"What man?"

Brewster threw a glance to the pea coat hanging on the chair Poppin was sitting in. "Inside pocket."

Poppin put down the knife and reached inside the coat. He fished out a folded piece of newspaper.

"Open it," the gruff old sailor said.

Poppin unfolded the newspaper clipping and looked at the photo. "Sherlock Holmes?" When he looked up Brewster was holding his knife in one hand and a pistol in the other.

"British officers don't carry German knives. Now you have some explaining to do."

"Easy old timer. I think we may have a common interest."

"I'll decide that. Go on. I'm listening."

"I work for a man who also has an interest in Sherlock Holmes."

"I have more than a little interest. He's responsible for sending a friend of mine to the gallows. I plan to return the favor. I've done enough talking."

"The man I work for would like nothing more than to see Sherlock Holmes get what he deserves."

"The man you work for? You introduced yourself as an officer."

"That is correct."

"Serving two masters, eh? Aren't that what they call treason? Who's the man you work for?"

"Best I not say. It's safer that way."

"Safer for you, or safer for me?"

"I like you, Mr. Brewster. Let's just say it will be better for both of us if my employer remains anonymous."

"Suit yourself. So, who's helping who? Are you helping me find Holmes, or am I helping you?"

"When it comes to Sherlock Holmes, my employer has eyes and ears everywhere. At the moment Holmes has gone underground, dropped out of sight."

"Doesn't say much for those eyes and ears does it?"

"Best you keep that thought to yourself, Captain. My employer is sensitive that way."

"I don't have time for this. If Holmes is out there I will find him myself. I don't need a toff like you getting in my way. Now, if you don't mind, I'd like to get back to sleep. This time without a knife at my throat."

"Sherlock Holmes is a resourceful fellow. That he has dropped out of sight most likely means he has something planned."

"I also have something planned, and Sherlock Holmes isn't going to like it."

"Holmes going underground is the type of thing that makes my employer very nervous. There is only one way to flush him out."

"Which is what?" Brewster thought for a moment. "Oh, you mean that silly sod he runs about with."

"Exactly. Dr. Watson. He will be our vector."

"Are we finished for the night? I'd like to get back to sleep."

Poppin rose to leave. "We shall continue our conversation tomorrow."

Brewster lifted his legs onto the bed and lay down.

"May I depend on you, Mr. Brewster?"

"You don't even know where Holmes is. When you find him, send me a postcard." Brewster rolled onto his side away from Poppin and pulled the covers over himself. "Turn off the lamp before you leave."

CHAPTER 23
Meeting again for the first time

The network of associates Holmes had cultivated over the years made it relatively easy to locate Miss Haas. She had checked out of her London hotel, booked passage on a train for Norwich, and then hired a taxi to take her to Cromer. We knew from the newspaper story Holmes had read in the future edition of *The London Times* Moriarty's plan for us would unfold in Cromer and Norfolk. Luring Miss Haas to Cromer was the first step. Whether Miss Haas was Moriarty's only mark or one of several possibilities, we had no way of knowing. By way of her editor, a Mr. Crisp, we learned Miss Haas had been invited to Cromer to interview for a potential writing assignment. Once Mr. Crisp was convinced our inquiry was a matter of utmost importance, his initial reluctance to provide information about Miss Haas's travels gave way to cooperation. Although he couldn't be certain, his sense was Miss Haas had not previously met the individual who had telephoned her. Ordinarily she would never accept a position without having met her employer in person, but the telephone conversation regarding the remuneration she could expect to receive was too generous to ignore. We thanked Mr. Crisp for his time and then considered our next moves.

"Holmes, how can Moriarty be sure we will travel to that part of the country? As I have yet to meet Miss Haas in the present, what would motivate me to travel to Cromer?"

"I have been struggling with that very thought, Watson. It is not unreasonable to assume I may have been observed reading *The London Times* in the Berlin Library."

"Which could mean Moriarty knows we know our fate is tied to Cromer and Norfolk."

"Possibly."

"And he is banking on the fact that we will do our best to avoid his trap."

"Unless—" Holmes appeared suddenly lost in thought.

"Unless what? What other possibility could there be?"

"Unless we are simply repeating what has happened before."

Good heavens. It was all simply too much. "Then we can do nothing to avoid our fate," I said with weary resignation. "What was written in the paper will come to pass."

"Keeping in mind we have the time dilation advantage."

"But Holmes, if we are simply repeating what has happened before, then we also knew of the time dilation before."

"Yes, it is all very confounding. Science and history can tell us a lot, but there are mysteries beyond our ken. The rational mind seeks answers in the midst of chaos. I cannot say with a certainty, Watson, that we have control over what will happen. But I refuse to be a pawn. I will not give Moriarty, the fates, whomever or whatever that satisfaction. Whatever those springs and motives that have been cunningly presented to us in their various disguises, I will not be cajoled into believing our course is anything but our own unbiased freewill and discriminating judgment."

"Melville."

"Hmmm?"

"You are quoting Melville."

"Albeit selectively and inaccurately. John, you know what you must do. Miss Haas must not be allowed to meet Moriarty. At all costs you must intervene and protect yourself."

"What will you do?"

"For the next few days you will be on your own for a while. I will be lying low for a time." Holmes took my hand and clasped it tightly. "Safe travels, John."

As I hailed a cab for Waterloo, Holmes disappeared into the fog. He had said he would be lying low. Of course I didn't believe that. Whatever Holmes had in mind, he didn't want me to be a part of. My role was to meet Miss Haas. Beyond that, I knew nothing. In due time Holmes would contact me.

I set out on my trip to Cromer with an unaccustomed anticipation and some slight apprehension. I had been smitten by Miss Haas, and I felt fairly certain she had been taken with me. But that was eighteen years in the future. Our circumstances were quite different here in the present. It seemed a long shot at best to think there might be a similar attraction. That I knew her and knew some few things about her gave me an edge, but I must confess that information made me feel more than a little devious. Was it fair of me to pretend we were perfect strangers? Holmes would have reminded me not to lose sight of our goal. Moriarty had to be stopped at all costs.

"Moriarty?" I said to myself. Suddenly a dark cloud moved over me. I had completely forgotten Miss Haas was an accomplice in Moriarty's scheme. Her interest in me had been a performance. She had pretended to know me only through newspaper photographs, when in fact we had met eighteen years earlier. Time had given her an advantage. Here in the present my hope was to reach her before she met Moriarty. Should I succeed, I would have succeeded in changing my fate.

Two and a half hours later I arrived in Cromer. Miss Haas was staying at the Hotel de Paris, an elegant yet oddly named hotel. Could one do anything but chuckle over the fact that one of Britain's most prestigious hotels bore the name of the French capitol?

I was shown my room, which more than met my requirements. After unpacking and a quick wash up, I ventured downstairs for a smoke and a drink. I must admit that I was as nervous as a schoolboy waiting for his first date. I couldn't be sure if Miss Haas would even visit the lounge. Perhaps I was hoping against hope. I checked my watch. After several drinks and no success, I told myself one more drink and that would do it for the evening.

Halfway through that last whisky, my hope of seeing Miss Haas again was realized. Had anyone been looking at me, they would have surely seen my jaw drop. I had last seen Miss Haas eighteen years in the future. She had charmed me from the moment I set eyes on her, captivating me with her elegance and arresting appearance.

Seeing her now, no description short of 'breathtaking' would be adequate to describe her. Even forearmed with the knowledge that our chance encounter had been anything but chance, I was still taken with her. If it were true that in three days Holmes and I had an appointment with destiny, I didn't have the luxury of being timid. I would have to be daringly bold.

After ordering a drink, Miss Haas took a seat by the fireplace, opened a portfolio and proceeded to review what I presumed to be articles and illustrations. Perhaps she was readying her resume' for Moriarty.

"Excuse me," I said, moving between Miss Haas and the light. "John Watson."

Miss Haas looked up at me without the slightest hint of recognition. "Have we met, Mr. Watson?"

"Not exactly," I said, offering my hand. "Actually, it's Dr. Watson. Dr. John Watson."

"*The* Dr. Watson?" Miss Haas said with a noticeable arching of her brow. She slipped her hand warmly into mine. I experienced that momentary feeling of déjà vu. I couldn't help but consider if one can actually experience déjà vu if an event has yet to happen. In less demanding times, perhaps I would ask Professor Einstein.

"Yes, I am *that* Dr. Watson."

"Lurlene Haas."

"*The* travel writer?"

"Yes, I am *that* Lurlene Haas."

We both laughed.

"Forgive me, I am afraid I am having a little laugh at your expense. I recognized you the moment you entered the lounge."

"Would you care to join me, Doctor?"

"Only if you will call me John, Miss Haas."

"Very well, John. But you must call me Annalise."

"Annalise it is." I took a seat opposite Miss Haas and summoned the waiter to refresh our drinks.

"Now then, John, it comes as no surprise that I recognize you. I believe I have read every issue of *The Strand.* I am quite a fan. But how is it you know me?"

"I too am a fan. As a regular reader of *Here and There*, I feel positively cheated when an issue doesn't feature one of your articles or a photograph of you against the backdrop of an exotic location."

"Listen to us, we must sound like a mutual admiration society."

"I really am quite the fan, so much so that I would like to hire you myself."

"That's quite a remarkable offer. I—" Miss Haas broke off. After a moment of introspection, she said, "This wasn't a chance meeting, was it, John?"

Miss Haas had seen right through me. "Mr. Crisp told me you would be here."

"That was rather indelicate of him."

"You shouldn't fault Mr. Crisp. I am afraid I insisted."

"Then you must know I am here to accept a previous offer of employment."

"Exactly. Which is why I have traveled all this way. I am most keen to hire you."

"I have already accepted the position. I couldn't possibly turn it down now."

"You could, and you should."

"Are you always so bold, John?"

"Only when I have to be. I will pay you double what you have been offered."

"That is most generous, but I really can't. My word is my bond."

"May I confide in you?"

"I suppose it depends on what you are going to tell me."

"The man you have an appointment to meet, he's—he's—"

"Yes?"

"He is a very bad man."

Miss Haas smiled, as if somehow I had flattered her. "John, you are surely exaggerating."

Neither Holmes nor I knew with a certainty if the man Miss Haas was supposed to meet was actually Moriarty or one of his seconds. In either case it didn't matter. Miss Haas was to be enlisted to lure me to certain doom. Why she was chosen, I had no idea. Under what circumstances we would meet, there was simply no way of knowing. As Holmes had said, Moriarty was playing on a much larger field than we. He had the benefit of years of planning, whereas we had only days to respond. We were very much at a disadvantage.

I could not afford to be recondite. "I have never sworn this oath before. But on the grave of my late wife, you must trust me. I swear I am telling the truth. You have no idea how much you will regret ever having met that man."

"Posh! You act as if the fate of the world hinges on this matter."

Oh, such irony. "I am afraid it does."

Miss Haas burst out laughing. "How can I possibly take you seriously?"

I was failing in my attempt to persuade Miss Haas. In the parlance of gamblers, I had to go for broke. "As a colleague of Sherlock Holmes, we have many connections to Scotland Yard and government authorities. I am prepared to have you arrested for your own safety."

After several moments of silence, Miss Haas demurred. "You are persuasive, Doctor. Very well, I agree."

"You do?" I asked incredulously.

"Yes, I agree. Now what does the position entail?"

"Excuse me?"

"The position for which you wish to hire me."

I had been so busy trying to steer Miss Haas down the right path, I forgot I had offered to employ her. "Oh, editing, and illustrations."

"You don't seem sure."

I felt perfectly awful lying to this marvelous woman. "No, I don't seem sure, do I? So let me be perfectly honest."

"I thought you had been."

"Truthfully? I don't have a position for you. I just need your assurance that you will not take the position you have been offered. I am not exaggerating in the least when I say lives depend on it. I wish I could go into further detail, but I cannot."

Miss Haas took my hand. "Ordinarily this is the point in a preposterous story at which I would stand, thank my host, and dismiss myself." She locked eyes with mine for what seemed several uncomfortable seconds. "I have always valued my instincts. I like to think I am a good judge of character. I shall not press the matter further."

I breathed a deep sigh of relief. "I know I have asked a lot of you. If there were some way to make amends—"

"There is. It begins with dinner."

"How does it end?" I asked in what I confess was completely out of character for me.

Miss Haas smiled. "Let us see how dinner goes. Shall we say seven?"

"I will meet you here."

As Annalise Haas made her exit, I thought my legs would buckle. My heart was racing. I was completely out of my element in the role of lothario. Perspiration began to appear on my forehead.

Twelve hours later Annalise Haas and I were on a train back to London. Our dinner together had been wonderful. More than that I shall not disclose. I had sent word ahead to trusted colleagues that we were to be met at Liverpool Street Station. Upon arrival I ensured that Miss Haas would receive around-the-clock protection. I bid her goodbye and promised I would be in touch as soon as possible.

For the moment I had kept Miss Haas out of the clutches of Moriarty. Now it was up to Holmes to hold up his end. Whatever he was up to, I was completely in the dark.

CHAPTER 24
Obit

"I thought this place looked a bit odd when I put ashore. What is it then?" Jack Brewster asked, entering the dilapidated structure situated curiously on the stretch of beach called The Great Eye.

"A count or a lord built it to entertain his lovers," Poppin said dismissively.

Brewster pushed a hand through his beard. "We here for a reason? This place have anything to do with Sherlock Holmes? I thought we was going to London. I've got a score to settle."

"Change of plan. We still haven't been able to track him. I'm sure he'll surface soon enough."

"Seems to me I've gotten hooked up with a bunch of amateurs."

"Careful, my good man. As I advised you previously, you'll want to keep those thoughts to yourself. Professor Mor—" Poppin caught himself. "The Professor will be arriving shortly. Best to make a good first impression. Come on, let's go up."

"Where to?" Brewster asked warily. "What, up there?"

"Follow me."

Jack Brewster followed Darden Poppin up a long spiral staircase to the top of The Folly. It came out onto the lookout Brewster had seen when he first arrived. "Out there," Poppin said, pointing into the dark. At first there was nothing to see. Then Brewster saw a blinking light. It was a signal light. A few minutes later a skiff came ashore. Two men hopped out of the small boat and stood at attention on the shore.

"What's this all about?" Brewster asked.

"There's a U-boat out there." Poppin said, looking toward the blinking light. "It's ready for The Professor to board. He will be making a short trip to Germany. He has some plans he wishes to share."

"What plans?"

"Nothing to concern yourself with."

"Not that it makes a lot of difference, but I do like to know who I am working with and what's going on."

"Your only concern is Sherlock Holmes."

"Wherever he might be."

The light from the U-boat began to flash again. This time the message was quite a bit longer.

"What's its saying now?" Brewster asked.

Looking intently out to sea, Poppin carefully slid his right hand into his coat pocket and wrapped it around a pistol. "It seems we have an impostor in our midst, Mr. Sherlock Holmes." With pistol in hand, Poppin turned quickly toward Sherlock Holmes in the guise of Jack Brewster.

The two men standing at attention on the beach below heard the report of a pistol. A moment later a body toppled from the top of The Folly and crashed with a horrid thud on the beach below. Switching on their torches, the two men rushed to the crumpled body. They stared at the lifeless body and then at each other. Darden Poppin was dead. Both men looked up. The man looking down at them was no longer wearing a beard. "I too understand Morse Code, gentlemen." Holmes aimed his pistol at the men below. "I am also an excellent marksman." The men dropped their torches and ran to the skiff, hastily pushing it back into the churning waters of The North Sea.

It wouldn't be long before Moriarty would arrive at The Folly. Discovering he had failed in his attempt to ensure my demise in Cromer, Moriarty would easily deduce Holmes and I were one step ahead. He knew Holmes well enough to know he would likely try to neutralize Poppin before the major had a chance to move against the great detective. Contacting the U-boat captain and instructing him to signal Poppin to be aware of any strangers was a brilliant move.

When Moriarty arrived at The Folly, Holmes was already on his way back to London. The U-boat he was to rendezvous with had already put to sea.

Two days later *The London Times* regretfully noted the death of Major Darden Poppin. Expressions of condolence were conveyed at all levels of government, a funeral with full military honors would be held, an enemy provocateur was suspected. In a separate incident, Arthur Lee, 1st Viscount Lee of Fareham and First Lord of the Admiralty announced the British Navy would assist in the search for a German U-boat that had reportedly gone missing just beyond British territorial waters. Berlin thanked His Majesty's government for its gracious offer of assistance, but reported that all of its decommissioned U-boats were accounted for, as an active U-boat in international waters would be a clear violation of the articles of surrender.

CHAPTER 25
Notes and symbols

I met Holmes the following morning at 221 B. He was unshaven and looked all the worse for wear. "Assure me Miss Haas is safe," Holmes demanded before bothering to bid me a good morning.

"Very safe, I assure you. She will be heavily guarded wherever she may go, but she will not see nor feel the presence of anyone."

"Excellent." Holmes reached for a cup of strong, Sumatra coffee.

Over the next half of an hour, Holmes methodically shared the details of his fatal encounter with Darden Poppin at Randall's Folly. What hand Mycroft had in alerting the admiralty to the German submarine and its subsequent sinking, Holmes could not say. Perhaps Mycroft had been persuaded by the visit of Peter Johns and Sherlock's insistence that Poppin was in league with Moriarty.

"Poppin and Moriarty were both traveling back and forth by U-boat."

"It would have been impossible for Moriarty to pass through any of the normal checkpoints." Holmes filled his pipe and put a match to it. "What Mycroft didn't know is his prized double agent was ferrying Moriarty back and forth."

"Why that location?"

"I presume that particular spot makes it difficult to detect a foreign submarine."

"We have no idea how much information Moriarty has passed onto the enemy or the damage he may have done."

"No. It serves no purpose to speculate about matters we cannot verify."

"Do you think we have thwarted Moriarty's plans?"

"No, Watson, I do not. We have no doubt disrupted his plans, but his ambition far exceeds whatever roadblocks you and I have thrown in his way. He will certainly redouble his efforts to get even. We must not let down our guard."

"There is something that troubles me about this, Holmes."

"There is much that troubles me, Watson."

"Now that Poppin is out of the way, the future he inhabited will have changed."

"Yes. Perhaps in ways not too terribly great, but it will have changed. I find it difficult to imagine that man I met in the train station will not have existed for the past eighteen years."

"And the newspaper articles?"

"I may only assume that were we to read that newspaper again, there would be no mention of the deaths of Dr. Watson and Sherlock Holmes. It never happened."

"Do you ever think about our other selves?"

"Indeed, I do."

"Are you not the least bit curious?"

"Very much so Watson. My curiosity is such that I have actually considered spying on myself. It would be fascinating to know what has become of us. It is almost irresistible."

"You qualified that statement, Holmes. You said *almost.*"

"The beauty of life, John, is that it unfolds for each of us in ways both predictable and unpredictable. The future is not ours to know in advance. It is to be lived and experienced, for good or bad. The future is a gift. How dull and uninteresting life would become if we knew what lay in store. What would be the purpose of getting out of bed each day if there were no surprises, no wonder of what lay before us. I am afraid Moriarty has stolen something from mankind. Not only does he know the future, he is attempting to change it. No man should have that power, just as no nation should have the power of that weapon so many are racing to build. No, John, we will let our other selves be. I prefer to imagine the possibilities rather than knowing the certainty of what is to come."

"What do you think Moriarty's next move will be?"

"With no way to reach present day Germany, he has no choice but to return to the portal. With Major Poppin gone and no previous relationship with Miss Haas, Moriarty will find a future very different from the one he left."

"We have no assurance things will have gotten better."

"None whatsoever. I believe we must return to the portal and give our friend Einstein one more try. Failing that, I have posted a cryptic message in *The Times*. When we arrive in Berlin, I shall send a similar cable to *The Times*."

"Two messages eighteen years apart?"

"Yes, old friend, the time has come to bring things to a head."

After Holmes had a wash and brush up, we hailed a cab for the Croydon Aerodrome. Upon our approach to the aerodrome by way of Plough Lane, our taxi was forced to halt. A fellow with a red flag waved for us to stop while a plane crossed Plough Lane on its appointed flight. In later years, the idea of an airplane crossing a major automobile thoroughfare would be regarded as preposterous. While we awaited the all clear, I considered the significance of that red flag. It was a warning. I couldn't help but wonder if it was also prophetic. Had I shared that thought with Holmes he would have laughed. Superstition he would have said. When one has fought on the battlefield, sometimes superstition is the only thing left to cling to.

We disembarked at the pub where Einstein and I had previously met Maddox Dayton. Creature of habit that he was, Mayday was at that same table in the corner with a fresh pint. Unshaven, unkempt, and his arm in a sling, he looked every bit like a man who had just survived a crash.

"Hello, Doctor," Dayton waved with his good arm. "What brings you here?"

"You remember Sherlock Holmes. We would like to engage your services for another trip to Scotland, assuming you're feeling fit. We will pay you handsomely."

"You were right, Doctor. The pain is excruciating." Dayton flexed his arm. "I need the money all right, but I don't see how I can."

"Quite right," I said. "Perhaps there is another pilot you trust and could recommend."

"What, to fly my old Gem? No, no, no, no! There's only one man I trust to fly Gem. That's you, Dr. Watson."

Holmes raised his eyebrows and threw a glance my way.

"I don't think I—"

"Doctor, you saved my life twice. You landed the plane and you treated my wound. I know you can do it. I trust you."

Half an hour later Holmes and I were airborne, he

in the forward cockpit and I aft. Holmes turned to me. "Watson, you simply amaze me. More so every day."

I saluted my friend and colleague. It wasn't every day Holmes paid me a compliment.

In a third of the time it would have taken us by train, Holmes and I were once again in Loch Naire. We secured Gem and quickly made our way from the meadow to the station. Our friend who warmed benches was at his post. Out of habit, I paid the man a pound note.

"Very generous, guvnor. What's this for then?"

"The other fellow that comes through on occasion, the tall, gaunt chap. Have you seen him lately?" Holmes asked.

"A few days back, but not recently. If I see him, shall I say you asked? Is there a message?"

"Yes, give him this." Holmes reached inside his coat and produced a copy of *The London Times*.

"Aye, aye, captain."

Holmes and I repaired to the clearing. A moment later we were standing again in that alley in Berlin.

Upon our arrival, we were immediately faced with the dilemma of where to overnight. We agreed it wasn't safe to return to The Blue House. Darden Poppin had not existed for the past eighteen years, thus there would no longer be a connection between he, Ingrid and Max. However, Moriarty knew we didn't know Berlin well and that we might try to return to The Blue House, as it was familiar. "Too risky. Moriarty may be desperate." Holmes said. "We shall overnight in the station. It will be crowded with passengers. We will be as safe there as anywhere."

Our jaunt to the station took about half and hour. Holmes instructed me to make myself comfortable. "I shall return soon," Holmes said.

"You're leaving me here alone? Where are you going?" I asked.

"There is a haberdashery around the corner." And with that, Holmes exited the station.

"A haberdashery," I said to myself. "At a time like this."

Next to me on the bench was a discarded newspaper. I rifled through the pages as if I were actually reading it. I knew a few words in German. Mostly I entertained myself looking at the pictures. This Hitler chap was unquestionably a silly looking fellow. Recalling that Wells had imagined he to be the German Charlie Chaplin made me chuckle aloud.

Twenty minutes later I detected a presence in front of me. It was a man wearing a long, black leather coat and a black fedora. My heart skipped a beat. I looked into the stern eyes of the face staring down at me.

"What do you think, Watson? How do I look?"

"Holmes! Good lord, what are you doing?"

"I need to send that cable to London."

"And that requires a black leather coat and a fedora?"

"I require the appearance of authority. Messages to London by ordinary citizens might attract unwanted attention. It shouldn't take long."

Holmes entered the station telegraph office. The clerk, who should have been paying attention, was so absorbed in a book he was reading he didn't bother to look up. "I need this transmitted to *The London Times* immediately," Holmes said in German, dropping the note in front of the young man.

Without bothering to acknowledge Holmes, the clerk quickly glanced at the note. "This requires authorization from—"

"Your name!" Holmes snapped before the clerk could finish his sentence.

The young man glanced up. His eyes widened. "I'll send it immediately," he stammered. Nervously he tapped out the message. "Will there be anything else?" Perspiration erupted along his brow.

"Your name!" Holmes demanded.

"F-F-F-F-Franz," the young man stuttered painfully, wiping his forehead with his sleeve. He appeared as if he would pass out.

"No, Franz, that will be all." Holmes clicked his heels together and exited the telegraph office. The clerk let out an audible sigh. His head fell forward, crashing with a loud thud onto the desk.

"Are you going to get rid of that silly costume?" I asked when Holmes sat down beside me.

"I don't think so. I rather like it. It seems to afford a generous measure of respect."

"Or fear," I chuckled.

Few people in the station made direct eye contact with Holmes.

A long and uncomfortable night on the station bench passed without incident. When morning arrived, I stared at myself blearily in the mirror of the men's room. I felt as rumpled as I looked. After splashing cold water on my face, I joined Holmes for a bracing cup of black coffee in the station café. There, Holmes carefully laid out his plan. I was to spend the day entertaining myself while awaiting Dr. Einstein's return to his apartment from a day's work. In the meantime Holmes would board a train for Switzerland.

I walked with Holmes along the station platform to his carriage. He offered his hand. "A lot is riding on this John. We are leaving a lot to chance."

Chance, the very thing Holmes hated.

"Good luck, Holmes. I shall see you soon."

Holmes boarded the train and I waited on the platform until the last carriage was out of sight.

For the rest of the day I took in the sights of Berlin. I was beginning to appreciate the city despite the ugliness that was governing it and the rest of Germany.

At six o'clock, I arrived at Einstein's Berlin apartment. Holmes' directions had been precise. As he advised, I took numerous side streets and went in the front doors of several businesses and out the back in order to lose anyone who might have been following me.

I climbed the stairs of Einstein's apartment building and knocked. Einstein opened his door, took one look at me, and slammed the door in my face. Through the door I could hear Einstein dialing the telephone and tapping furiously on the cradle switch. "Damn!" He said, slamming down the phone. The door reopened. "What?"

"Can we talk?"

Einstein made a sweeping gesture for me to enter. He slammed the door closed behind me. "Good lord, what is it with you two? You never give up. We have nothing to talk about. For the last time, Doctor, I will not betray my country. Why must you persist in this? Have I not made myself clear?"

"Perfectly."

Einstein launched off into a veritable barrage of German, none of which I understood. His arms flaying and his hair standing straight up, he looked positively certifiable. His tirade went on for several minutes before he finally calmed down. I think he must have exhausted himself.

"All we are asking is that you consider the possibility this may not be the future that was intended."

"Enough of these silly time travel stories."

"Doctor, you are the one who came up with these theories. Are you not the least bit curious? Have you not for one moment considered this is not the reality that it should be?"

"Doctor Watson, this *is* reality. What has happened or did not happen in the past matters not one iota, because we are *in* reality. Nothing that has happened can be changed."

"I agree completely," I said. "Do you mind if I sit?"

Einstein shook his head. "You do?"

"Yes. Nothing that has already happened can be changed. However—"

"No!" Einstein blared. "I know where you are going with this, and I don't want to hear it."

"Your problem, Doctor, is you have no faith in your own theories. You work out the mathematics and the science in the abstract, but you never believe in the concrete."

"I am Einstein, Dr. Watson!"

"And you have my deepest admiration and fullest respect."

"Now if you will excuse me, I have work to do."

"Very well!" I pulled myself up out of the chair. "One last thing before I go, I have something for you."

"What is it?"

"A gift from your past."

From inside my coat I removed the pocket watch the young Einstein had given Holmes. I held it by its chain, allowing it to dangle and spin. Einstein was momentarily hypnotized as the famous inscription E=MC2 revealed itself every other turn.

The great scientist took the watch from me. "I lost this watch years ago. How did you get this?"

"From a friend of yours, in the past."

For a moment Einstein seemed to have been drawn back in time. Then reality returned. "Is this supposed to convince me of your preposterous story?"

"I don't know, Doctor. What I do know is that you have changed very little over the years. You and your younger self are hard headed. Holmes and I have tried desperately both here and in the past to convince the two of you of the existence of the portal. I am hoping we have succeeded with that younger fellow, which is why he gave us this prized possession to present to you as a last ditch effort. The rest is up to you. You are entirely correct, you are Einstein, but if working with Holmes has taught me anything, it is that intellect without imagination is not intellect at all. We have done what we can, Doctor. Goodbye. I have a train to catch to Berne."

"What is in Berne?" Einstein asked.

"Reichenbach Falls."

CHAPTER 26
Berne

The overnight train from Berlin to Berne took twelve hours. I felt fortunate to have a compartment to myself. Exhausted as I was from the awful night I had spent in the Berlin station, I resisted falling asleep. Our encounter with Miss Erikson was still fresh in my memory. It was impossible to discern if I had been followed or not. In truth, I would not have been able to tell one of Moriarty's men from the German secret police.

Daylight was beginning to appear behind the Alps as the train pulled into Berne. I exited onto the platform, cast a cursory glance about to see if anyone stood out in the crowd and then hired a taxi to take me to the Reichenbachfall Funicular. A little more than an hour later, the taxi deposited me at the foot of the quaint little railway that climbed to the top of the falls. Unexpectedly a flood of emotions gripped me. It was here I had said goodbye to Holmes. That we were returning to the site of that dreadful encounter filled me with trepidation.

It was early. The funicular was not scheduled to open for another two hours. Holmes had instructed me to wait for him. Perhaps because of my experiences of late, I sensed I was becoming less inclined to be a man of patience. Jumping back and forth through time made one realize how precious time is. To waste time was to waste life.

Of a sudden a man wearing a long leather coat and black fedora appeared. My heart skipped a beat.

"Watson, old chap. You made it."

"Good lord, Holmes, you gave me a start. Take off that silly outfit."

"Sorry, old friend. But it has rather allowed me to move about freely. The assumption that I am secret police has proved most useful. No one searching for Sherlock Holmes looks twice at me. If anything, ordinary Germans avoid making eye contact. Such is the power of these secret police. They are nasty fellows these Nazis, Watson." Holmes removed the coat and hat and stuffed both items in a refuse bin, joining me on the bench where I had been sitting while awaiting his arrival. "My disguise has served its purpose. Now, tell me, how did your meeting with Doctor Einstein go?"

"I thought the watch would do the trick, but it was not to be. He will not be dissuaded."

"I feared as much. I hoped we would not have to take the next step, but we are faced with no choice."

"Holmes, how can Einstein be so blind?"

"Watson, the German people are being fed information by an extraordinarily sophisticated disinformation machine. One does not easily turn against one's own country, not even a man as brilliant as Einstein. We have tried our best with the Professor and failed."

Holmes wasn't one to dwell on failure. In the likelihood that Einstein could not be persuaded, we would move on to a bolder and far more daring plan. Holmes had already set the wheels in motion.

"Holmes, can we be sure Moriarty will take the bait?"

"I am counting on the Professor's love of the theatrical, not to mention a return engagement to match wits with Sherlock Holmes. Here at Reichenbach, Watson? It is surely an attraction the Professor cannot resist."

"I hope you are right. Have you been to the top?"

"Yes. A great deal has changed. Since we were here last, a small footbridge has been built across the falls, linking one side with the other. Given your rendering of my encounter with Moriarty years ago, I gather that narrow footpath you so ably describe in your narrative became a tourist destination. No doubt it was deemed much too dangerous for visitors. Short of declaring the area off limits, a footbridge seemed the best alternative."

Perhaps I had been a little too descriptive in my account of that meeting.

"I believe the footbridge will prove an excellent spot for our tête-à-tête with the Professor. When the time is right, you will take the funicular to the top."

"But, Holmes, the railway doesn't open for two more hours."

"We shall open it ourselves."

"What about a driver?"

"That task has fallen to you, Watson."

"I don't know a thing about driving a tram."

"Watson, you flew a plane from London to Loch Naire. You can surely operate a train. It is really quite simple." Holmes slid open the door of the car and stepped inside. "Just pull this handle and off you go. The train will stop automatically when it reaches the top. The handle will lock itself into place."

"What about you?"

"I will go on ahead. I fully expect Moriarty will be there when I arrive. He will have taken the trail from the other side of the bridge. It is less traveled, affording him some measure of stealth. It will take me approximately one hour to reach the top. Once I arrive, hopefully our wait will not be long."

"What if he doesn't come?"

"There are few certainties in life. If he doesn't come, then we shall be forced to improvise a new plan. See you at the top, old friend."

Holmes entered the trailhead and set off on foot for his journey to the top of Reichenbach Falls.

I made myself comfortable in the driver's seat of the funicular and dutifully began my wait as Holmes instructed.

An hour later Holmes reached the small pedestrian bridge that joined one side of the falls with the other. Below the bridge the mighty falls cascaded into a raging whirlpool of churning water.

Entering onto the bridge, Holmes spied another figure approaching slowly from the other side. Both men drew on to each other, each pausing well short of center to take the measure of the man standing opposite.

"Sherlock Holmes," the other man said. "After all these years. I must say it is a pleasure to see you again. And such a well-chosen location."

"Hello, Professor. I thought you would be pleased." Although this man was his nemesis, Holmes had always felt a certain respect for the intellect of this master criminal.

"Your message in the classified section of *The London Times* was irresistible. Quite amusing. How could I possibly resist an invitation to revisit the site of our battle to the death lo those many years ago? Such flair, so theatrical, so operatic. But I must say, you look extraordinarily healthy. You seem hardly to have aged at all. No ill effects from our last meeting?"

"A lengthy period of recuperation, followed by the strict regimens of a healthy diet and exercise. I have recovered exceptionally well, thank you. You seem no worse for wear, Professor."

"Indeed. Were it not for a fallen tree that had tumbled into the falls, I would not have the pleasure of this conversation."

"You are fully recovered?" Holmes asked.

"Quite, but I suspect your real interest is where have I been and what has occupied my time since last we met?"

"Of course."

"I think of myself as a citizen of the world. For obvious reasons, it is difficult for me to settle in one location. The law has a long memory, Mr. Holmes. I spend my days painting, traveling, and reading."

"Nothing else to occupy your time?"

"Oh, you mean have I been up to anything nefarious? I had rather hoped this meeting was to be a social occasion, two old friends reminiscing over old times, but I see now that is not the case. No, my friend, those days are far behind me. I have retired."

"I am afraid Scotland Yard would take a decidedly contrary view."

"Most assuredly, which is why my travels unfortunately no longer allow me to return to that most wonderful of cities. But please, Mr. Holmes, we are avoiding the obvious."

"I have only recently come to appreciate that one never really leaves the past behind. However we might try, the past is impossible to escape. What we were, we remain."

"Riddles, Mr. Holmes?"

"The world is in a precarious state, Professor. I am afraid Germany is traveling down a horrible path."

"Indeed. These are not easy times for a man such as myself to move freely. Forgive me if I fail to see how the politics of Germany have a thing to do with me. Whatever I may have been responsible for in my past, you give me far too much credit if you believe I am somehow in league with the despots who imagine a thousand year Reich."

From a distance came the sound of turning gears and the clink, clink, clink of the Reichenbach Funicular slowly making its way to the top of the falls.

"The last time we met at this spot, Professor, you and I assumed a mantle of importance to which we were not entitled. We met as the champions of a world whose fate depended on the outcome of our petty contest."

"Good lord, Holmes. You do go in for the dramatic. You thought our meeting was a contest between the forces of good and evil? I ascribed no such hyperbole to our meeting. I rather looked upon our meeting as the opportunity to rid myself of a thorn in my side."

"This time, I am afraid the fate of the world does hinge on what happens here."

The funicular was now in sight.

"Sometimes you are a very confusing fellow, Mr. Holmes. I am at a complete loss to understand your meaning."

"I invited you here today because there is someone I would like you to meet. He is coming now."

"I see. You were stalling for time."

Holmes turned toward the funicular as it came to a stop a few meters from the bridge. When he returned his attention to Moriarty, the Professor was holding a pistol.

"You disappoint me, Professor. I had hoped we would be gentlemen about this."

"Insurance, Mr. Holmes."

I glanced at my watch. "He's late," I mumbled to myself. I wasn't sure how long Holmes could hold off Moriarty before something drastic happened. From my vantage point at the base of the falls, the pedestrian bridge was barely visible. I couldn't be sure Moriarty was present.

My attention turned to the sound of feet shuffling along the wooden platform beside the funicular. I expected to encounter Professor Moriarty from 1921. I did not expect to see Jane Wells with him.

"Good morning, Doctor. You don't mind that I brought along a companion, do you?"

The younger Moriarty stood behind Jane Wells with a pistol pointed at her back.

"I am sorry, Doctor," Jane Wells said.

"Jane, are you all right?"

"He came to our home, locked Herbert in the basement, and said he needed me for insurance. He tied me up, gagged me, and stuffed me into an airplane. He is perfectly despicable."

"You have no idea, my dear."

"I am not your dear," Jane bristled.

"It was most thoughtful of Mr. Holmes to leave a copy of *The London Times* with our friend at the Loch Naire station, but as I had already seen a copy well in advance of my arrival at the portal, I was able to make alternate plans."

"Was it necessary to abduct Mrs. Wells?"

"Holmes really didn't think I would come without some measure of protection, did he? Please, Mrs. Wells, climb aboard." Moriarty pushed Jane onto the seat beside me and then took a seat behind us. He kept the pistol aimed steadily at our backs. "To the top, Doctor."

I engaged the gears of the funicular. The tiny train slowly began its ascent to the top of the falls. As we drew near, Holmes and Moriarty came into view, standing a few meters apart in the middle of the footbridge. The train slowed automatically, coming to a stop in the tiny station adjacent the falls.

Moriarty waved his pistol for Jane and me to exit. A small trail with boulders on either side led to the entrance of the bridge.

"Here he comes now," Holmes said, "the gentleman I thought you would be intrigued to meet. It is someone from your past."

Jane and I entered onto the bridge.

"Mrs. Wells," Holmes said, appearing a little more than surprised. "I hadn't expected company."

"He saw the paper before leaving London," I said.

"The best laid plans, Mr. Holmes," the younger Moriarty said. "You have also invited a guest, I see."

Holmes turned to the elder Moriarty. "Professor Moriarty, meet Professor Moriarty."

The two men regarded each other for a moment.

"Illusions, Mr. Holmes? Theatrical tricks?" The elder Moriarty asked.

"I assure you, the man you are seeing is very real," Holmes said.

"You must explain yourself, Mr. Holmes." The elder Moriarty said.

The younger Moriarty answered. "Mr. Holmes has discovered a scientific anomaly that allows one to travel into the future from the past. He is of the mistaken belief that my future self will dissuade me from the course of action I have chosen to follow."

"Now I see," the elder Moriarty said, addressing himself to Holmes. "It is my younger self to whom you were referring previously. It is he who has insinuated himself into the affairs of Germany."

"Indeed, he is attempting to shift the balance of power in favor of Germany in anticipation of the coming war. I had hoped to appeal to your intellect. You surely realize nothing good can come of the evil designs of a mad man."

"I will pretend you are speaking of Adolph Hitler rather than the man I see before me now."

"Of course," said Holmes.

"Well played, Mr. Holmes," said the younger Moriarty. "Very convincing, however, your transparency betrays you. Your purpose is exquisitely clear."

"What purpose is that, Professor?"

"You imagine I am unfamiliar with the Pauli Exclusion Principle. There can be no other reason for your bringing the two of us together."

Upon hearing those words my heart sank. Moriarty was always a step ahead.

"And now you understand my desire for insurance," the elder Moriarty said, indicating the pistol in his hand. "I respect your intellect, Mr. Holmes, but I never trust you. By the way, I too am familiar with the exclusion principle."

The younger Moriarty moved past Jane and me toward the center of the bridge, nearer his future self. "Whatever you think you have accomplished, Holmes, your problems have just doubled."

"Holmes," I asked, lowering my voice, "is this what you had in mind?"

"Not quite, old chap."

"Are we quite finished, Mr. Holmes?" The elder Moriarty asked. " I believe I speak for myself and myself when we say you are becoming quite tiresome. This is your last bow."

"Shouldn't we return to the portal first?" I said to the younger Moriarty, attempting to stall for time. "Recall, you were the one who said you couldn't be sure what might happen if someone from the past were killed in the future."

"We will take our chances, Doctor. It is time to bid all three of you adieu."

I slipped my arm protectively around Jane Wells. "Don't hurt the girl. She has nothing to do with this."

"Nothing to do with this?" The younger Moriarty turned toward the elder Moriarty. "She has been nothing but a royal pain in my side since the moment I first laid eyes on her. I will toss her off the bridge right after I toss off you and Sherlock Holmes."

"You tosser!" Jane Wells screamed, breaking free of my protective arm. Before the younger Moriarty could react, Jane lunged at the man and sent him reeling toward his older self. The two men caromed into each other. At the very instant the two men touched, bullets fired in each direction, miraculously missing all of us. That was followed by a blinding flash and then an otherworldly sound unlike any I had heard before or since. An instant later an explosion followed hard on. And then all went blank. What happened after that is impossible to relate.

The next thing we knew, the three of us were staring into that mighty abyss. The force of the explosion had ripped the tiny bridge asunder. It was completely torn in two. The side on which I had last seen the elder

Moriarty jutted skyward, twisted and mangled, rising up as if it were a snake about to strike its prey. The side on which Holmes, Jane Wells, and I had stood was equally as twisted and mangled, only our side of the severed bridge arched obscenely toward the falls, as if a giant tongue trying to lick the roiling waters hundreds of feet below. Underneath our half of the shattered bridge the three of us clung to a surviving beam. Below us the churning waters of Reichenbach Falls thundered angrily. We held on for dear life, I on one side, Holmes opposite, and Jane Wells between.

There was no sign of either Professor Moriarty. At the point of sounding indelicate, I hoped they had been blown to hell. No matter what the fate of the world, it would be better without Moriarty.

"Einstein will no doubt be pleased to know The Pauli Exclusion Principle is more than a theory," I yelled, straining to be heard above the deafening roar of the falls.

"We have Jane's quick thinking to thank for that," Holmes added. "You will understand if I don't shake your hand, Mrs. Wells."

"Please, Mr. Holmes, this is no time for formality. Call me Jane."

"Very well, Jane. Dr. Watson and I owe you our lives."

"We are faced with quite the predicament, Holmes." I wasn't sure how much longer any of us could hold on.

"Indeed, Watson, this is a tough nut, I must say. Perhaps the most difficult of any test we have faced."

"I am not ready to give in yet," Jane Wells cried. "We haven't come this far to be so easily defeated."

Jane Wells had an uncommon strength of spirit.

"Nor I, Jane," Holmes said, suddenly sounding resolute in the face of what seemed to be certain death.

"Any thoughts on how we escape, Holmes?"

Holmes thought for a moment. "That, dear Watson, I think we really must call *The Final Problem*."

AFTERWARD

"And so there we were—left hanging."

I reread that final sentence. Should I add more? Was it appropriate to end a Sherlock Holmes adventure with a cliffhanger? I should let my editor decide. For now it would do. I added the end punctuation and typed THE END. No sooner had I added those final words than Holmes entered my apartment and lowered himself into a chair.

"Hello, Watson!" he said cheerily.

I rolled that last page out of my typewriter and set it upside down on the stack of pages to my right. "Holmes, I was just thinking of you. How is retirement?"

"Words fail me, Watson. I simply cannot express myself."

If my friendship with this man over the years had taught me anything, it is that bees, gardens, and afternoon strolls could never mollify a mind as restless as his. "You hate it, don't you?"

"Unbelievably so. I am bored stiff." His eyes fell upon the manuscript. "Hello, what's this? Writing again?" Rising from his chair, he approached my desk and turned over the ream of pages. "From the future case files of Sherlock Holmes. Future case files, Watson? There are no new case files. You have covered all of our cases."

"I am trying my hand at something new: fiction. To be more precise, science fiction."

"You don't say?"

"Yes, now that we are both retired, I thought our adventures might take us in a new direction."

"I would much rather real cases than imaginary adventures. You have yet to put title to page. What is the name of this one?"

"I believe I shall call it *Sherlock Holmes and the Portal of Time.*"

"Shall I guess? We travel into the future to save the world."

The wind positively left my sails. "How on earth could you possibly guess?"

Holmes strolled toward the window and looked down at Baker Street teeming with cars and buses and people. As in my novel, London was on the mend again, only this time a World War later.

"Elementary, my dear Watson." We have just come through a World War unlike any one could imagine. Historians will mull every decision and every move for ages to come, wondering how such a cataclysm might have been prevented. I daresay that is where your thinking has taken you. As I continue to be the subject of your adventures, I am reminded of the immortal words of Herman Melville.

A mighty subject must have a mighty theme.

John H. Watson, London, 1946

Also from MX Publishing

MX Publishing is the world's largest specialist Sherlock Holmes publisher, with over a hundred titles and fifty authors creating the latest in Sherlock Holmes fiction and non-fiction.

From traditional short stories and novels to travel guides and quiz books, MX Publishing cater for all Holmes fans.

The collection includes leading titles such as *Benedict Cumberbatch In Transition* and *The Norwood Author* which won the 2011 Howlett Award (Sherlock Holmes Book of the Year).

MX Publishing also has one of the largest communities of Holmes fans on Facebook with regular contributions from dozens of authors.

www.mxpublishing.com

Also from MX Publishing

The Missing Authors Series

Sherlock Holmes and The Adventure of The Grinning Cat
Sherlock Holmes and The Nautilus Adventure
Sherlock Holmes and The Round Table Adventure

"Joseph Svec, III is brilliant in entwining two endearing and enduring classics of literature, blending the factual with the fantastical; the playful with the pensive; and the mischievous with the mysterious. We shall, all of us young and old, benefit with a cup of tea, a tranquil afternoon, and a copy of Sherlock Holmes, The Adventure of the Grinning Cat."
Amador County Holmes Hounds Sherlockian Society

Also from MX Publishing

The Detective and The Woman Series

The Detective and The Woman
The Detective, The Woman and The Winking Tree
The Detective, The Woman and The Silent Hive

"The book is entertaining, puzzling and a lot of fun. I believe the author has hit on the only type of long-term relationship possible for Sherlock Holmes and Irene Adler. The details of the narrative only add force to the romantic defects we expect in both of them and their growth and development are truly marvelous to watch. This is not a love story. Instead, it is a coming-of-age tale starring two of our favorite characters."
Philip K Jones

www.mxpublishing.com

About the author

Michael was born in London. As a lad he lived in Salthouse for a time. In those days The Rocket House was still standing. Thanks to the Town of Salthouse, the history of that unique structure has been preserved. Later Michael moved to the U.S. These days he divides his time between Alaska and Florida. His previous works include several plays, which may be found along with additional information at www.playsbymichaeldruce.com. *Sherlock Holmes and the Portal of Time* is based upon his play of the same name, published by Dramatic Publishing.

www.ingramcontent.com/pod-product-compliance
Lightning Source LLC
Chambersburg PA
CBHW070007260626
47159CB00005B/1701